LISTEN, YOU STINKING FREAKS. LISTEN, IF YOU WANT TO LIVE! IN ONE MINUTE I'M GOING TO FIRE THAT ROCKET. IF YOU STAY YOU'RE GOING TO *BURN*, GODDAMN YOU. START RUNNING, SCUM!

The *FOE*men had said that one way or another they would prevent Hentson from defiling Earth with alien technology—with their bodies, if need be. They had also said that "Jesus" Hentson would stop at nothing. Now they *believed* it.

by JOSEPH GREEN

ace books
A Division of Charter Communications Inc.
A GROSSET & DUNLAP COMPANY
360 Park Avenue South
New York, New York 10010

STAR PROBE

An ACE Book

Cover art by Boris

First Ace printing: December 1978

Printed in U.S.A.

PART I

From the Master's Thesis scrapbook of Jarl Hentson

MAN AND SCIENCE COLLIDING?

by Marc Charney

(Associated Press)

STAMFORD, Conn.—Man and science are on a collision course—and it is Man who will have to change, says the winner of the Nobel Prize for physics, Dr. Dennis Gabor.

'I distrust the nature of Man for very good reason,' Gabor said. 'He was made to fight his way out of the forests, but it's doubtful he was made to live in a highly civilized society.'

Man's impulses to fight and grow, Gabor says, lead to tremendous problems in an age of science—problems of overpopulation, pollution, destructiveness, and restless boredom if there is too much leisure time.

The way out, he says, is not to eliminate science—but to change Man's motivations. Scientists and educators can work together to turn men toward excellence as a goal instead of more material goods; toward a better quality of life instead of destruction, he added.

Gabor, a 71-year old native of Hungary who moved to England while Hitler's power was growing, won the 1971 Nobel Prize for inventing holography—a laser beam system for reproducing three-dimensional images without lenses.

But he also built a reputation in academic circles as a philosophic writer on the implications of science, particularly the problems it poses for society and the solutions it may be able to come up with. . .

Science, he says, has helped create problems of a calamitous order in the twentieth century. Gabor says nuclear war probably won't come in this century, but overpopulation and pollution could prove disastrous within a generation.

'Man,' he said, 'is a fighter, and he's restless. Workers are now bored, dissatisfied . . . It's not starving proletarians who are doing the striking now; they prefer an unpaid holiday, protesting. I can't blame them for that—the work they are doing in industry has become too monotonous for their intelligence to take.'

The answer, he says, must be a society in which Man's impulses to grow and fight are rechanneled into creative activity that solves social problems.

'The problem is to convince people—particularly young people—to put as much energy into the slowing down of the system as they have into its growth.'

From *Today* May 4, 1972
(Florida's Space Age Newspaper)

1

Sunday, June 5, 2011

In the middle of the Sunday afternoon movie the holovision well suddenly faded from view.

Harold Hentson glanced up in annoyance. He had not been watching the three-dimensional figures above the floor projector but was following the dialog. It kept his mind occupied while he lay sprawled on the resilient rug, patiently correcting Jarl's attempts to insert triangular pegs into round holes on the training board between them.

A new projection formed in the well. It was the life-sized figure of a man, standing before a waist-high newsperson's console. He was looking across its inward-tilted face to his unseen audience.

Harold stared at the lined, serene features of Alfred Murray, chief newscaster for World-Wide News. The old man glanced briefly at his console, then raised his eyes to the world. 'We interrupt your regular Sunday programming for a newsflash of extreme interest. The Space Benefits Agency has just released a report from MoonEye, its recently completed observatory on the back of the moon. At 1:00 this afternoon, astronomers detected an unidentified light about two billion kilometers out in space, between the orbits of Saturn and Uranus. This light is moving with great speed, on the order of eight-thousand kilometers a second, and appears headed for Jupiter. While no astronomer we have contacted will commit himself, all agree this is very unlikely to be a natural phenomenon.'

Murray relaxed slightly and leaned forward over his console. His deep baritone sank to the confidential rumble in which he reported gossip and rumor, or gave his own opinions. 'Fellow world citizens, the scientists know what this puzzling light *must* be; and before long they'll have to admit it! Our own experts tell us nothing but a spaceship could produce a light of that intensity or move with such tremendous speed. Our solar system is about to be visited by something—or someone!—from another star system. Unconfirmed sources report that MoonEye has already focused its largest radio telescope on the stranger and is trying to make contact. Some of the brains at SB think this must be an unmanned explorer, of the same type they proposed building last year. You may recall the WorldGov Council rejected the idea after extensive debate.'

Murray straightened up, and his eyes returned to his hidden console screen. 'WWN is staying in constant touch with the Press Office at Space Benefits. We will return with an update as soon as more information becomes available.'

The fatherly, trustworthy face faded from view, and the movie returned.

Harold rested on one elbow and ignored the pegboard, lost in thought. The unexpected news was stunning in its implications. A confirmed visitor from another solar system . . . One of the oldest dreams of Man, contact with another intelligent species, fulfilled at last in 2011 . . . It seemed inappropriate for so important an event to occur during the quiet peace of a Sunday afternoon, while he lay playing training games with his retarded son.

Jarl made a whimpering sound. Harold smiled at the husky nineteen-year old, reached for the next peg, and handed it to him. The younger man took it and began studying the board with idiot intensity. Harold leaned back and waited, repressing a sigh.

* * *

When the movie returned, Jodie Carson touched the remote control by the relaxor and turned off the Tri–D set. She leaned back against the chair's springy but yielding resistance, and it slowly adjusted to the new posture. For once the newsflash had been a genuine surprise, something totally unexpected.

After thinking for a few minutes, Jodie rose from the chair and crossed to the visiphone. She punched out a number, then placed her right hand on the glass in the face of the cabinet beneath. The door popped open. She reached for a small plug-in unit, then looked up at the screen. A familiar face stared impassively back at her.

'Hello! Want to scramble with number three before we talk?'

'Sure.' The other woman reached down to open her own cabinet. Jodie inserted her unit in the scrambler slot. The screen dissolved into a patchwork of swirling color patterns but cleared a few seconds later when the circuit was completed on the other end.

'Strobe, did you catch that newsflash from WWN about five minutes ago?'

'Sure did, Sarcoma. That's a weirdie. Think it's true, or is WorldGyp up to something sneaky—as usual?'

'Good question. That's why I called. Will you alert our people at Kennedy and RI, tell them to see what they can learn? I was coming down next Friday for the Hernandez rally, but if this is genuine I'll shuttle down tomorrow. It could hurt us.'

'Oh?' asked Strobe, lifting long blonde eyebrows.

'Last year we barely managed to kill that idiot plan to build interstellar space probes. Now if someone has actually sent one to *us*—the idea of returning the message may be hard to fight. And there are too many hungry children in South America for us to let WorldGov burn up still more billions on useless space programs.'

'Hadn't thought of that. In fact hadn't thought much about it. Whole thing's kinda' weird.'

'Call me as soon as you get a confirmation it isn't just a big fakeout. And I'll probably see you tomorrow.' Jodie gave the blonde a warm smile as she reached for the scrambler. Strobe was a nothing in the head, but she had been a good member of the antitechs for many years.

Jodie looked around her apartment. She had been inside for four days, working hard on two stories for FOE, the official organ of the New Friends of the Earth Society. She could finish the second one tonight and leave the manuscripts with the editor tomorrow on the way to the air terminal.

So now the poor tortured Earth was to be visited by a rocket from outer space! Just when they were finally making real progress, actually winning most of the really important battles in the WorldGov Council, the suffering citizens were to be exposed to new and highly advanced technology.

Or were they? If the visitor was unmanned, an automated probe of the type SB had wanted to build—perhaps it would simply fly by and disappear. And then those who cared about this rotten old world could get on with the business of trying to save it.

* * *

Robert Brown appeared in the rec room door, caught Harold's eye, and waited. Harold nodded slightly. The muscular physical therapist crossed the room and put out a hand to Jarl, who obediently got to his feet. Jarl stood several centimeters taller than Robert and was in almost as good a condition. The therapist led him to the adjoining exercise room. The door was opened, and Harold saw Robert leading Jarl through an opening series of weight-lifting 'games'.

Harold turned off the holovision, opened the curtains, and stood staring down twelve floors to the ocean. Low, lazy swells were rolling in off the Atlantic, whitecaps breaking above their long green bodies. The beach was crowded, as always in June on a Sunday afternoon.

It had been a bitter disappointment last year when the WorldGov Council turned down the SB proposal to build and launch a series of interstellar probes. The space sciences community had backed the project almost world-wide, but the environmentalists and antitechs had combined to kill it.

And now a probe or spaceship had entered the solar system. The Earth was on the receiving end of an exploration. So intelligent life elsewhere in the galaxy was confirmed, and a new era dawned. Man was no longer alone, and the future might hold startling new dangers or undreamed of promise.

These were large thoughts, but perhaps this was the time for them. And from the practical viewpoint, it was also time to reassess the situation. Could a renewed effort to build Earth's own probes now succeed? And if so, could Rockets International beat the monopoly charges leveled at them last year and get the contract?

Harold realized he was jumping too far ahead. First it was necessary to learn more about this unexpected visitor, and its intentions.

In his study, Harold closed the door and visied Goldstone on RI's private channel. He did not recognize the alert face of the young engineer on the screen but saw behind him the Operations Room of the Complex. The office force was home on Sunday afternoon.

The engineer obviously recognized Harold; his eyes widened slightly. 'Shift supervisor Grant Scott here, sir. May I help you?'

'Hello, Grant; glad to meet you. Did you fellows hear the WWN broadcast on our visitor in the outer solar system?'

'Yes sir; we'd gotten it two hours earlier, direct from MoonEye.'

Harold cursed mentally, without letting his expression change. This man had no way of knowing what his company president considered important. 'What is the Big Dish on just now, Grant? Can we pull it off, say once an hour, and pick up on the visitor for five minutes?'

Grant hesitated, thinking hard. He finally said,

'I think so, Hal. Contractually the time is obligated to the Pluto Project, but the spacecraft doesn't require continuous coverage.'

'Good. Then please establish a tracking program, and send my office twelve-hour reports. If it isn't broadcasting, try to get velocity and trajectory figures out of MoonEye and plot us a course. I want to know where it's going and when it will arrive. I'll have Pete Dawson contact your manager tomorrow to make it official. Also—please do this on the side, and keep it quiet.'

'Your request is official enough for us, Hal. We'll get started right away.'

'Fine, Grant. Then tell the night shift I'd like the first report on my desk in the morning.'

'You'll have it,' the engineer promised. Harold said good-bye and broke the connection.

Leaning back in his chair, Harold frowned at the ceiling. For the thousandth time since his father had died four years ago, he wished he could ask the old man's opinion. The first Jarl Hentson had founded Rockets International, though he only ran it four years before leaving to become President of the United States. He had been a man with a mind both practical and visionary, an unusual combination of dreamer and doer.

A vague desire that had been nibbling at the edge of Harold's mind for several months suddenly ate its way through. There *was* a way to communicate with his father, providing he was willing to accept a degree of danger to young Jarl. And with the advent of this unexpected visitor in the solar system, that price no longer seemed too high.

Lily had emerged from her suite and was watching the movie on the rec room holovision set.

Harold tried to speak to her, but she lifted a finger for silence. He shrugged, went to his own quarters, and changed into bathing trunks. Ten minutes later he was swimming hard against the incoming waves, working his way out into deep water.

* * *

Monday, June 6, 2011

'Helloo, Jodie; got something for us?' asked Eugene Jones, dragging his lanky two meters to his large feet. His old-fashioned glass-topped desk was littered, as usual, and he was ignoring the waiting work while reading a sex FacSheet.

Jodie took the two manuscripts from her travelbag and tossed them on the waiting heap. 'Gene, someday the rest of the board is going to agree with me that you've got to be replaced. And then maybe we can get an issue of the Bulletin out on time one month.'

Jones grinned, large yellow teeth shining through red-bearded lips. He admitted to being lazy and undisciplined. The tall young Harvard dropout was also a brilliant though erratic editor and one of the few paid professionals on FOE's staff.

In the identity she had established for her reportorial work, that of alternative press writer Jodie Carson, Jodie served on FOE's board of directors. Many people in the organization knew she was also the fiery protest leader Sarcoma. But no one at all knew her real name was Judy Karlson, and that her father was the millionaire head of the Karlson Kompany.

'I've often wondered how a woman so petite and

pretty on the outside could be so large and tough on the inside,' said Jones, the grin vanishing. 'I'd also like the address of the Goodwill store where you buy your clothes. But let's not fight. Instead, why don't you take me to the Holo LightShow tonight in Merritt Park? Peruski has a Trojan War sequence in the programmer that features a twenty-meter Hera doing the Temptation of Zeus. It should be *sextraordinaire.*'

Jodie frowned; she *would* have enjoyed a new Peruski sequence. He was one of the few LightShow artists whose gigantic creations seemed real and alive when they appeared in the air. Holo projection could recreate the gods and make them believable despite their outsized immaturities.

"I'll be out of town. And while I'm gone, why don't you get your mind off sex and do some work for a change?'

The tall man's flirtatiousness vanished. Jones sat down and picked up her articles. 'Don't worry your lovely head over it, little Cancer; I'll get both of these into the next issue.'

'Thanks for nothing,' said Jodie and then turned and walked out.

The New Friends of the Earth had its headquarters in a delapidated old building on Congress Avenue in Chelsea. It had been established there after the old California group died of internecine warfare. Most of the prior members had joined the new organization, but a sizable number said the new FOE did not represent their views and had refused. The present FOE had only a few thousand members, but they were all highly dedicated environmentalists.

As Jodie walked the four blocks to the Personal

Rapid Transit Station on Park Street, her anger slowly subsided. When the deadline approached, Gene Jones would get to work. His problem was that he seemed unable to take his mind off sex until the need to attend to business was overwhelming.

There was a ten-minute wait for the next PRT car. She spent the time in deep thought. Since Strobe had called earlier and said the visitor was undeniably real, and very likely an unmanned probe, she had been wondering how best to counter the impact on the public. Jesus-Son-of-God-Hentson would surely crank up RI's public relations staff and start a new drive to build interstellar rockets. And that was a program Space Benefits had conservatively estimated at eighty billion dollars and ten years time—all to be shot away into space and forgotten.

Probably the most effective approach would be to turn the technologists' claims around, say the fact that Earth had been found first killed the need to send out messengers of their own. Yes! That idea could be sold. She worried at the thought as she boarded the small white car with three other passengers, found Logan International on the lighted map overhead, and fed the four-digit number into the simple keyboard. When the last passenger punched in her destination the little car took off, accelerating smoothly up the gentle incline to the twin suspension rails. Almost immediately it turned off Park on to Pearl Street, following the thoroughfare to the McArdle Bridge, where it crossed low over the dirty brown water of the Chelsea River. Then it was down Meridian to Maverick, stopping three times to change passengers, and on to the Logan station. There she had to switch to the airport bus, which took a small group to the South Terminal. And twenty minutes later she boarded the small Coastal Shuttle feeder jet and strapped in.

With takeoff and landing time included, the subsonic feeder plane took an hour to reach JFK. But the feeders flew only to Shuttle terminals, and her ticket was already punched for Miami. Jodie walked direct from the jet to the Shuttle and claimed her reserved seat.

The two hydrogen-fueled jets in the tail of the delta-winged Shuttle flared to life. The 200-passenger craft taxied to the runway. Jodie ignored the routine voice of the host, explaining the life-jacket procedure as a pretty girl fitted one on. A Shuttle sank like a rock if it went down in the water.

The flight over the Atlantic to Miami was uneventful. At almost four-thousand kilometers an hour top speed, it was also short. Once, just for the hell of it and to spend Karlson Kompany money, Jodie had ridden a Coastal Shuttle around the full circle. It took a long day. Going south, the first leg was this trip from New York to Miami. Then it was over the Gulf of Mexico to Houston, and through the air corridor across a virtually deserted section of Northern Mexico to Guaymas. (The stop in Mexico was the price the USA had paid for the air corridor.) From there the ineradicable sonic boom battered a strip of land across the Baja California peninsula, then went overwater to Los Angeles. After that it was up the Pacific to Seattle, and overwater again to Anchorage. The next leg was over thinly settled northern Alaska and the icy tundra of the Canadian Northwest Territories. There was a last landing at St. John's in Newfoundland, and then it was home again to New York. Next day you could fly that route in reverse, if you wished.

In Miami Jodie rented a steamcar at the airport and headed north, via the Everglades Throughway. The new road cut through the heart of the great swamp to the broad shallow waters of Lake Okeechobee and the sprawling complex of truck farms that surrounded it. Bridges were frequent, to permit a slow but massive flow of water to the south.

Jodie drove slowly, her eyes savoring the vast sweep of wind-rippled water and sawgrass, the occasional hummocks covered with low trees, the tranquil, brooding immensity of this uninhabited land. She always came this way when leaving Miami. The calm and peace of the scene, broken only by heavy traffic on the Throughway, invariably refreshed and invigorated her.

But more had been accomplished here than the preservation of beauty. When earlier environmentalists had stopped the relentless southward march of the truckfarmers some thirty years back, they had saved the lower peninsula for the eighteen million people who now lived there. From Ft. Myers on the west coast to Ft. Pierce on the east, the tip of Florida was almost a solid wall of condominiums and apartment buildings. Most were inhabited by elderly people on fixed incomes. The only practical and cheap source of water for such a multitude was the Everglades. But the ancient swamp had been swiftly disappearing down man-made drainage canals, with new farms sprouting on their banks like tropical weeds. That rape of the great natural reservoir had ended; no new land had felt the plow's bit since 1980.

Jodie wondered how many of the millions eking out their lives in their tall, sun-warmed mausoleums knew of the debt they owed to the old Friends of the Earth. If not for them, Florida would have long ago reached its saturation point. Like most of the world, the retirees probably took the water that flowed freely into their homes for granted.

But a lack of appreciation and understanding was nothing new for environmentalists. They worked from conviction, not in the expectation of praise. Fortunately, many people realized where their long-term interests lay and supported groups like FOE, whether or not they actively participated.

It was growing dark when Jodie reached Cocoa Beach. Feeling tired, she drove directly to Strobe's apartment. The tall, muscular woman met her at the door, wearing a sympathetic expression and carrying a cold glass of vitagin.

'Welcome, far-traveler! Rest the bottom in a relaxor and I'll tell you the latest. It's good. Jesus Hentson really *does* think he's the Son of God. Only he's got his mythology a little twisted. He wants to bring his old man back, not ascend to join him. Could you believe in the resurrection of Jarl Hentson?'

Jodie could only stare at her hostess as she sank wearily into a chair. 'Are you serious, Strobe? How can that be?'

The husky woman smiled. 'A little something I knew about, but not enough to spread the word. Jarl Hentson isn't totally gone. Not even death can relieve the world of a US President, these days. His mind has been preserved on tape and is ready to spring forth at the urging of the mighty computer. And today Harold Hentson called in the company physiologist and asked him how long it would take to bring the old man back.'

The door chimes tinkled, and Strobe admitted two of the local FOE group, both young women. Strobe introduced Jodie as Sarcoma, and their eyes widened.

The younger of the two impulsively crossed the room as Jodie rose and hugged her. Surprised, she allowed the embrace. The second girl, more shy, hesitantly extended a hand. Instead of taking it, Jodie patted her cheek.

'I'm Inez Rogers,' said the young one, who could not have been more than eighteen. 'And this is Cynthia; Cindy Holcomb. Oh, we've been hearing about you for *years*! . . . but isn't it dangerous for you to come out of hiding? I mean the incitement-to-riot charges and all. . .'

'I'm not wanted in the US,' Jodie said, smiling. 'Unless we run into some zealous cop who wants to try extraditing me, I'll be fine.'

'Cindy works in Jesus Hentson's headquarters computer room,' Strobe volunteered. 'I asked her to stop by and tell you what she knows.'

Cindy was a thin, fragile girl with delicate features and very long black hair. Inez was a sturdy, freckle-faced redhead. Both were well-dressed, which was a relief to Jodie. No matter how dedicated one might be to the movement, scruffy and smelly compatriots could become tiresome in a hurry.

The new arrivals seated themselves. 'What I have to tell really isn't all that much,' Cindy began. 'Today before lunch Pepi Austurio—he's the company physiologist and an old friend of Hal Hentson's—came in and checked out all the tapes on President

Hentson's brain-reading. There was a whole bunch of them, just boxes and boxes. We don't issue the series without a signed order from Mr. Hentson. Pepi didn't have one, so he had us vise Hal, and he said go ahead.'

Jodie frowned. 'I'm completely lost. How can you bring back a dead man from a bunch of tapes?'

'Well, I'm not a computer engineer, just a programmer, but I know a little about that,' Cindy went on, her voice growing more confident. 'In 1998 someone came up with a gadget, a kind of improved electroencepholograph, that could read the actual currents flowing through the brain. There are lots and lots of circuits there that are permanently fixed. This machine analyzes all the established paths and produces patterns, in a kind of electronic matrix. It knows to ignore all the muscle controls and autonomic functions, things that just run the body, and concentrate on the memory, the thought centers, and the info you have stored in the cortex on the frontal lobes. The computer has to tape all this in a linear form, but you can play it back into a bit machine's memory banks, actuate all the circuits at once, and produce something they call a persona, a kind of simulation of the original brain. It's terribly expensive, and ties up a computer for several days, so it doesn't get done very often. RI just has the tapes because Hal insisted the government make him an extra set when they read old Jarl Hentson's brain.'

'I wonder why we haven't heard more about this,' Jodie asked, her voice thoughtful.

'It takes months to do that original reading,' Cindy answered. 'And the US and WorldGov haven't publicized it because too many people are conceited enough to think their memories and thought patterns should be preserved for future generations. I've heard that the US President before Jarl was the first to be brain-read. Since then it's spread, including the last two WorldGov Premiers, a few famous scientists, and so on.'

'That's certainly very interesting news,' Jodie said. 'Look, do we have anyone—not necessarily an antitech member, just a friend—who works with the RI computer? We should try to keep an eye on its schedule, learn what Asturio's assignment is.'

'We can do that,' said Cincy. 'There's a girl in Pepi's lab I bowl with who'll tell me. But why would Hal want to bring his father back?'

'I don't know,' Jodie admitted. 'But let me remind you, before Jarl Hentson formed Rockets International he was a highly experienced astronaut. The first man on Mars, and all that. Maybe Jesus Hentson wants to consult with his father about this Probe.

'Find out what you can and come back tomorrow night,' Jodie went on, rising. 'I'm glad to have met both of you—and perhaps we'll be working together before the week is over. Now I've got to drag it off to rest, or I'll collapse right in front of you.'

She was not really that tired but felt a need to be alone to think. Harold Hentson had to be up to something—but what? In any case, you could bet it would be for the benefit of RI and technology—and against the welfare of the average citizen. And somehow it connected with this strange visitor from outer space. It was a good thing she had caught that newsflash and hurried down here.

2

Tuesday, June 7, 2011

'Hal, here's the latest tracking data and analysis from Goldstone.'

Harold glanced up from his cluttered desk. He took the sheaf of paper from Pat Pajick, his executive assistant. 'Did the fellows who ran this know to keep it quiet?'

'Per your instructions, our manager at Goldstone was told to hide this work in his budget. Space Benefits doesn't know, and officially it doesn't exist.'

'Fine; thanks, Pat. Now call Raoul Stone and build a fire under him to get that weight/acceleration trade-off study finished. I want it ready by staff meeting time tomorrow.'

Pat raised carefully plucked eyebrows. 'Raoul just visied me with a status report. He has about two days work left. If you want this ready by nine tomorrow, he and his team will have to work all night.'

Harold hesitated. That was a rough requirement to lay on his engineering staff—especially when he had no certainty the information would be used.

'Hal, the noon news will be on in a minute. The expectation among the newshawks is that the WP will announce WorldGov's decision in regard to the Probe.' Pat hesitated, a troubled look on his smooth young face. But when he resumed, his soft baritone was calm and well-modulated, as always. Pat had never been known to raise his voice in anger or impatience. 'May I suggest we catch the broadcast before you decide?'

'Yes you may,' Harold said, touching the button that caused a Tri–D screen to rotate out of the desk surface into the upright position. Harold switched to the commercial news channel as the screen brightened. Pat drew up a chair without waiting to be asked.

Harold had gone through three assistants trying to find a suitable one. He had first noticed Pat Pajick in the Contracts Department, where he had risen very rapidly to Manager's Assistant—then stalled for three years. Pat was a brilliant man but had little force or drive. He was destined to operate always in the shadow of a stronger personality, where the necessary head-on confrontations could be endured by someone of tougher fiber. A genuine argument literally demoralized Pat Pajick for several days. Therefore he never argued.

The screen swirled in a riot of blending colours, then cleared. It was a commercial. Harold flicked the sound down and watched impatiently as some determinedly happy adolescents romped through the gawdy attractions of TeenTown, USA. Then the calm and dignified face of Alfred Murray looked out at them, and Harold turned the sound back up. He could not endure hearing commercials. Thank the stars Rockets International, which did not sell to the general public, advertised only in the technical FacSheets.

'The big news of the day so far is the decision of WorldGov not to intercept the Probe.' Murray announced in his soothing rumble. 'Yes, the emergency session just concluded accepted the recommendation prepared by World Premier Hsi Wu and his staff. The WP reasoning, in short, is that when dealing with the totally unknown it is safest to take no action at all. Another good reason is that this would be a suicide mission if we *did* send out an astronaut. Some preliminary calculations by the people at MoonEye indicate we could probably rendezvous with the Probe, but there would be no power left for the return trip. No one in government is suggesting we make such a sacrifice. The scientific community feels certain the Probe is only a complex unmanned spacecraft, of the kind WorldGov has considered sending out—but so far has been unable to afford. The suggestion by Conservative Party Chairman Phillips that we meet it in space with two or three fusion bombs has been rejected. While no one thinks it will take hostile action against us on its own, quite a few people feel it may have defensive weapons—and no one wants to see them used. The astronomers are busy focusing every available radio and optical telescope on the Probe, to learn what they can while it's with us.'

Murray moved on to the next item, and Harold turned off the set. He felt a little sick, even though the decision was expected. When the potential dangers and gains were equally unknown, government always took the course of least resistance.

'I'll tell Raoul to keep his people over tonight and finish that study,' Pat said as he headed for the door.

Harold nodded and picked up the smuggled report from Goldstone. RI operated the old facility under a management contract from Space Benefits. The WP and his people had examined similar data and considered meeting the Probe with bombs, which was easy enough to do—but had they studied the more difficult idea of capturing it?

Harold did not think so.

But Harold Hentson, president and major stockholder of Rockets International, could at least satisfy his curiosity. The question of whether it was technically feasible to attempt a capture of the Probe had occurred to him Monday, when it seemed established that the visitor was unmanned. He had immediately asked his VP for Research & Developing Engineering to determine the maximum velocity that the largest RI rocket could attain with a small payload.

Harold glanced briefly through the thick computer runoff from Goldstone and settled for the analysis. This was the third one since he had asked for twelve-hour reports. There was nothing new, but the uncertainty factor had fallen sharply, down twenty percent since the last one. The Probe was still steadily decelerating. The change that had upped the analysts' confidence was a small course correction. This had placed the visitor in the exact path needed to lose maximum possible velocity while swinging around Jupiter, providing the next target was Earth. It was now down to 100th light speed. Assuming the known rate of deceleration continued until encounter, it would pass Earth at a speed of less than 400 miles per second.

Harold saw with wry amusement that someone had carefully translated the figure into kilometers-per-hour for him: 2.3 million. The fact he was not a physicist like his illustrious father was well known at Rockets International.

After separating the summary. Harold tossed the rest of the paper into his reclaimer. The parts were falling in place. If the staff meeting in the morning produced the answers he expected, he was going to be confronted with the most important decision of his career.

Harold was accustomed to tough decisions; he made them every day. But a wrong one here could cost him his job, and he enjoyed being president of RI too much to take risks lightly. Yet the potential here was so great it was worth a gamble against high odds. This might be one of those times when only the boldest action could succeed, when anything less meant certain failure. And though no one but himself would know it, he would be haunted for the rest of his life if he failed this chance through lack of nerve.

One vital item still missing was an astronaut willing to bet his life on what was probably a suicide mission. The preliminary information available to Harold indicated the odds were heavily against a safe return home—if there was any point in going at all.

Harold called Pat in and gave him the task of finding a willing astronaut by meeting time Wednesday. He authorized a payment that made Pat's eyebrows lift again.

Harold's visicom trilled, but before he could answer it Pepi Asturio walked in unannounced. The short and pudgy physiologist hurried to the desk and laid a thin blue notebook on the highest stack of paper. Pepi could ignore the secretaries outside because he was a personal friend. He was smiling broadly, white teeth flashing against his darkly olive skin. 'Hal, we can do it! Give us young Jarl tomorrow, and Friday you can talk to your father again—or at least a pretty complete reincarnation of him.'

Harold pushed back, stood up, and stretched. Cramped muscles cracked and popped with the effort. 'Okay, Pepi. Set it up to get started tomorrow, immediately after the 9:00 staff meeting. I'll bring Jarl in with me in the morning.'

Pepi gave him a slightly puzzled look. 'Hal—you realize we don't know how the imprinting will work on a long-term basis. This has never been done except with a computer analog of the brain. And that isn't, and can't be, a complete simulation. I think the probability is high that the patterns will fade after a few weeks.'

'Pepi, my best guess is that two weeks will be enough time—if we go through with this at all. We'll know more after tomorrow.'

Pepi nodded and left. Harold picked up the blue notebook and read as he ate lunch. Knowing his president's penchant for short summaries, Pepi had hand-written his results and compiled them at the rear. What the study proved, in essence, was that the complete persona stored on reel after reel of tape could be imprinted on a human brain in three days time. How effective the transfer would be, no one could say.

The original intent of brain-reading was to store the mental patterns of valuable individuals in as complete a form as possible. But the previous US President, Arnold H. Zimmerman, had been resurrected in a computer two years ago and asked for his advice. The artificial personality had produced an answer—which was then ignored by the World-Gov Council.

Pepi was certain the imprinting could be performed on a human brain and result in a better simulation than that afforded by the computer. Even the largest machine did not have the number of circuits available in the human cortex. If it had been done in practice, though, the results had not been announced.

But bringing his father back, valuable though that keen and experienced mind could be, was not Harold's most pressing problem. The need for an experienced astronaut was the weak link in the chain he was forging, the one most likely to pull apart. He had one more expedient available if no one volunteered, but it was a desperate, last-gasp answer, not to be attempted until all else failed.

At present Harold was trying to hold open all options, analyze all possibilities. He had been president of RI for seven years now, becoming at thirty-four the youngest man to hold the post. (Even Jarl Hentson had been forty-five when he assumed the presidency of the predecessor company and changed its name.) And the one management technique he had pounded into his head, time and again, was to look down all possible roads before choosing one—and if necessary, to build a new road!

Harold stepped outside his office, into the large reception room shared by Pat Pajick and two secretaries. He waited until Pat finished the current call, then asked, 'What do you think the odds are?'

Pat turned in his chair. 'About a thousand to one. And there are only seventy astronauts qualified to fly the Big Bird.'

'Keep trying. Do you mind staying over tonight

and seeing if you can reach a few at home? I'd like the count to be as complete as possible.'

'Sure, I'll stay. But if I reach half, and they all flatly say no . . .' Pat shrugged and turned back to his visiphone.

Harold had no trouble completing the unspoken thought. *The second half would say no also!* You had to be crazy to volunteer for a suicide mission where the chances for success were minimal—and an insane astronaut was a contradiction in terms. Their mental health was as rigorously checked as the physical.

Harold had kept his morning schedule clear of appointments, but the afternoon had to be devoted to running Rockets International. The day passed swiftly as he attended to routine business, and he left for home at 4:00. Pat was still patiently, doggedly running down the list of seventy astronauts, repeating RI's offer of a million dollars American to any volunteer. So far no one had even seriously considered it.

The bright Florida sun was beaming down on the roof of the RI Executive Tower. While he waited with a growing crowd for the aircar, Harold glanced over the flat countryside towards the Atlantic, almost ten kilometers to the east. He could make out the tops of the condominiums lining the ocean along New Smyrna Beach, including the one built by RI where many executives lived. The Hentsons resided a kilometer to the south, in an older but more elegant structure.

The next aircar landed and Harold hurried aboard, jostling elbows with other headquarters personnel who were going east. One of his first acts as president had been to abolish the private aircar

RI executives had been using for years. The act had not gained him any popularity with his associates.

The distance was short to the first stop in New Smyrna, but the automated aircar landed on every tenth tower. Harold was drawn into conversation with two pretty personnel specialists who were interested in his opinion of the Probe. That seemed the universal topic since the announcement from MoonEye Sunday afternoon.

'Hal, did you hear that WorldGov has announced they're going to just let the Probe go by without trying to destroy it?' asked the younger of the two, a slim and willowy girl dressed rather modestly in a white stretch-skin suit.

Harold nodded. He hadn't met either woman, but it was a common custom at RI to call him by his diminutive name.

'Well, don't you think that's the sensible thing to do?' asked the second woman, who was apparently trying to make an impression on the boss while she had the chance.

'I'd rather hear your opinions than give mine,' Harold answered them both.

The older woman nodded. 'I've heard you were like that Hal, that you would rather listen than talk. But that isn't fair! Your information is certainly better than ours.'

Harold had to agree. 'Sorry; you're right. Okay, it's my opinion that WorldGov should make every possible effort to *capture* the Probe. The technilogical gains from being able to study an interstellar rocket should be enormous.

The willowly one opened large eyes even wider. 'Oh, I *agree* with you! I said that during break this afternoon, and everyone thought I was off my rocket. Wait till I tell them tomorrow!'

'Guess I lost that round,' said her friend, with a trace of impish humor. The truth was not going to impress the boss. 'Wanda *did* say that, and she was about the only one. The rest of us felt trying to capture it might be dangerous. What if it has some sort of death-ray, with maybe orders to defend itself? For all we know it could wipe out the Earth!'

Harold's stop saved him from having to answer. He said goodbye and hurried to the express elevator, rode down twenty floors to the street, and walked the last few hundred meters to his building. On the twelfth and last floor he pressed his right hand on the glass admittance panel and stepped inside when the door swung open.The Hentsons occupied the entire top of the building.

Lily hurried in from the kitchen. 'Hal! You're home early. Get out of your clothes and I'll bring you a drink.'

Lily Brewster Hentson was a tall, regal woman with silver hair and a figure just tending toward plumpness. She came from a family that had been rich since the American civil war. They had met at World U and married in Harold's freshman year. Lily had dropped out to have young Jarl and never returned. It was one of the several things she held against her husband.

'Thanks, darling. And then stick around, please. We have to talk.'

Lily gave him a slightly puzzled look but nodded. They had very little to talk about these days.

As he changed into a loose one-piece lounging outfit Harold found himself wondering for the thousandth time why he had not terminated the contract with Lily. She had enough money to be independent. They hadn't shared sex in more years than he could remember, and their lives had diverged sharply since the birth of Jarl Hentson the Second.

And perhaps that was the answer. Lily had steadfastly refused to have another child, out of fear the unknown malady might strike again. Instead she devoted all her time to young Jarl. For at least seventeen years now it had been painfully obvious he was not going to grow mentally, that he would always hover somewhere on the dim border of extreme retardation. But Lily had refused to acknowledge their son would always be a mental baby, although he still had to have help feeding himself. At least he had finally been toilet-trained, after several painful years.

At first Lily had worked with the full-time therapist and nurse for long hours, exercising her son's healthy body and trying every known technique to force the crippled mind to grow. She had pointed out each slow bit of progress to Hal, claiming eventual triumph. Over the years the claims had gradually died away. Now they seldom discussed their son. The nurse had long since vanished, but the physical therapist remained, a permanent part of the Hentson family. He had his own quarters both in the condominium and in the country home in the Great Smoky Mountains of North Carolina.

Harold had never had the nerve to tell Lily her slavish devotion to young Jarl was a form of self-indulgence, a withdrawal from all challenges except that one. She had been failing in school when she withdrew. Lily simply did not like to study. Money had insulated her from all turmoil, every common form of struggle. At a certain point she had stopped trying to grow, accepting herself as she was. As an adult Lily was a compliant, undemanding woman, easy to live with but dull company. And over the past few years she had spent less and less time with their son, tacitly accepting that he too had reached his limit. Most of her daylight hours were passed watching holovision, where she enjoyed many lives—all once removed from the hard jaws of reality.

Lily returned with Harold's favorite drink, an exotic concoction of fruit juices flavored lightly with rum, and seated herself on the divan before the glass wall. Harold moved to join her. Outside and below, the beach looked cool where the westering sun threw the shadows of the row of buildings across the white Florida sand. A crowd of bathers, most from the condominiums but also vacationers and tourists, enjoyed the mandatory one hundred meters of beach between buildings and water. Modest bathing attire was back in custom at the moment, and all the men and women Harold could see wore one-piece suits of brightly colored stretch-skin. It was a pleasant, serene view, just the kind Lily enjoyed. She never walked that one hundred meters of beach herself but often watched the crowd.

'Hon, do you remember a few months back when I mentioned the possibility of creating a computer persona of my father? And I said, just in joke, that it would be nice if we could create the old Jarl in the young Jarl's head, since it isn't being really used now.'

Lily immediately looked defensive. 'Of course. And I said Jarl may not have much intelligence of the type you measure in tests, but he's a very sweet and nice boy, and you shouldn't joke about things like that.'

'Yes, you did. Well, I *was* joking, at the time. But now we've learned it may really be possible to do exactly that. A great deal of new information on brain-reading and imprinting is available now, and it seems it's quite practical to plant a computer persona in a human brain. I want to try it with Jarl, Lily. It can't hurt him—and Pepi tells me we should get a much more complete personality than we could create by using a computer.'

Lily went from defensive to alarmed. 'Hal! You can't be serious! Why how could you even *consider* letting someone tamper with Jarl's poor damaged brain? Absolutely not! I forbid it!'

'I could consider it because the effect is temporary. Jarl will be himself again in three or four weeks. He will be perfectly safe, there is no danger, and it might even be good for him.'

Lily seldom argued with her husband. She accepted the fact she was no match for Harold in a contest of wills. But though her interest in improving young Jarl's condition had waned, the protective feeling was still strong. 'You just said all this is new. You can't be absolutely certain it won't hurt Jarl, no matter what Pepi says. No, Hal; you leave my son alone.'

'He's my son too,' Harold said, his voice very low.

'No! no! no! no!' Lily said very rapidly and started crying.

Harold leaned back, relaxed, and waited. After five minutes he started slowly and patiently repeating that the treatment wouldn't hurt Jarl, it would be temporary anyway, and it was desperately important that the senior Jarl Hentson be restored long enough to help Harold with a serious problem. Lily continued to shake her head, though the weeping eased. Harold assured her over and over that he would never do anything to hurt their son, that her fears were groundless, and added that this might be Jarl's one chance to make a genuine contribution to the Hentson family.

And after a long two hours of argument, tears, and near-hysteria on Lily's part, she gave in, as both had known she would from the beginning.

3

Tuesday, June 7, 2011

While Strobe was at work Tuesday Jodie spent the day on the visiphone, primarily gathering information. She also got commitments from the local leaders of several antitech groups in the Orlando area. If bodies were needed, they would be available. A demonstration could be arranged anywhere in central Florida, almost on demand.

Cindy Holcomb came over after dinner, face alight with exitement. 'Sarcoma, you won't *believe* this! Pepi Asturio reserved the engineering computer for tomorrow through Friday—and the lab techs are converting a brain-reading cap to work the other way! After work I called Robert Brown—he's the physical therapist for the Hentson's retarded son—and Robert said he has orders to gather enough clothes and things to last the boy for three weeks! He'll be staying in the RI laboratory.'

'My God!' Jodie said softly. 'He's going to bring his father back by using his son's brain!'

'It's the only thing that makes sense!' Cindy went on, still excited. 'And I have another hot story. One of the girls who delivers mail to Hal's office heard his assistant, that weird jellyman Pat Pajick, talking to several astronauts this afternoon.

He was offering each one a million dollars to intercept the Probe, and explaining that it would probably be a suicide mission. Of course he isn't getting any takers.'

'Far up and out!' muttered Strobe.

'Even if RI does find an astronaut willing to try it, WorldGov has just made a decision not to interfere with the Probe,' said Jodie, thinking aloud. 'I don't see how even Jesus Hentson can buck that. Let's wait it out a few days, while keeping a close eye on RI.'

'You don't know Hal Hentson,' said Cindy, her voice firm. 'If he decides to go after the Probe, SB and WorldGov and all the rest won't stop him. And I don't understand why we should, either. What harm will capturing the Probe do to the earth's ecology?'

Jodie gave her an amused look. 'Nothing, directly. But don't you realize the aerospace lobby would immediately start clamoring to build an armada just like it? Think of how many people that would tie up in the totally useless project of shooting a bunch of rockets off into the galaxy! We've already wasted a tremendous amount of human time and energy sending unmanned spaceships to Uranus and Pluto, and the rest of the planets. What has it all gotten us? Absolutely nothing! For that matter the entire space program has always been just one long gravy train for aerospace companies and fat-assed government bureaucrats. I say it's long past time we started devoting our energy to improving the earth we live on! Think what we could have accomplished with all those billions of dollars!'

Jodie had automatically moved into the raised voice and emphatic statements of the practiced orator. Cindy was looking at her rather oddly. Jodie laughed and relaxed. 'Pardon me for getting carried away, Cindy. It's just that I've fought the space waste so long the idea of seeing it get even larger sets me off. Believe me, any impartial analysis of the space program will show the costs to be huge and the return small. Going to the moon in the first place was just a national prestige thing. We can't afford such "prestige" today.'

Cindy nodded, though she did not seem entirely convinced.

* * *

Wednesday, June 8, 2011

'Okay, Raoul, let's have it,' Harold Hentson said to open the meeting at 9:01. Each of the eight persons around the table had a cup of hot stimcaf at hand, and vitabread was available in small plates.

Raoul Stone looked tired—he and his team of top engineers had worked through the night, as expected—but his voice was firm and clear. 'We can do it, Hal, but just barely. With a small load like one person and his life support, we can pull a steady three G's out of a Big Bird for close to twenty-two hours. If the Goldstone analysis holds up, we'll need less than eighteen for the intercept. That leaves four hours to play with, for contact and a trajectory change for both. Not having the exact mass of the Probe, we can't give a definitive answer on whether it will be enough. Our best guess is yes.'

Harold nodded and looked across the table at Carson Jamison, VP for production. 'If I give you the go-ahead now, can you have the cargo out of that vehicle and convert over to a single pilot launch in eighty hours? Requirements are full ground control, and life support for a minimum of six weeks for that one man. Also, we'll have to build some sort of attach fitting for the nose.'

Jamison thought it over for several seconds. Finally he said, 'Close; a little too close. Give me eighty-eight hours.'

Harold knew Carson Jamison was a cautious man. He had probably estimated he could do it in sixty-five or seventy hours. Ground control was built in and only required activation. Removing the folded parts of the Space Station, still under assembly in unoccupied areas, was a routine operation. The huge double tank which formed the bulk of the vehicle could be filled with liquid hydrogen and oxygen in a few hours. These were intended for in-orbit refueling of the Lunar Shuttle and the Lunar Lander. But the single huge engine that powered the vehicle also drew on the propellants in those tanks, and could do so until they were empty.

'Can we live with that, Pete?' Harold asked next.

Peter Dawson was VP of the Tracking & Control Divison, in constant touch with his personnel manning Goldstone. He was a lean, skeptical man of sixty, accustomed to dealing with the unyielding realities of celestial mechanics. He touched long smooth fingers together and gave a carefully studied answer. 'Hal, we are dealing with two major assumptions here, neither of them verifiably true. First, we are assuming the Probe will stop its engines some predetermined distance from Jupiter—we're working with ten radii—to minimize interference with the instruments during the actual fly-by. It would do the same again at Earth. Second, we assume the Probe will use this planet to regain some of the velocity it's shedding, and do the same with Saturn on its way out of the solar system. The present line-up of the three make this possible, and so far the Probe has behaved exactly as a computer-directed explorer would—picking a flight path that utilizes planetary gravity and motion to conserve its own fuel supply. Now if the engines stop and start exactly on schedule—and it seems safe to assume their thrust is an invariable—we can plot an intercept point between here and Saturn where we can match velocities with it. But we have to launch eleven hours before it reaches Earth, and we have no assurance that it *will* swing off toward Saturn. As for the answer to your specific question—eighty-eight hours is running down to the wire. The Jupiter encounter starts in a few minutes, and we plot it at one hundred and fourteen hours after that before it reaches Earth.'

Harold nodded. 'Thank you, Pete. Carson, we will have to better that figure. Let's try for seventy-five hours. And for the rest of this discussion, let's postulate that the Probe will behave exactly as Pete said. Pat, please report on the search for a pilot.'

Pat Pajick cleared his throat. He did not enjoy speaking before this group of strong-minded executives. 'Hal, I have contacted fifty-six of the seventy qualified astronauts. Not a single one seriously considered our offer. Most were simply unwilling to go against the decision by WorldGov. The rest declined when they learned the odds were high against returning alive.'

Harold nodded. 'Sensible people all. Very well. Let's consider the alternative of an *unqualified* pilot. If we go to a primarily ground control mission format, leaving only the actual rendezvous maneuvers up to the man on board—Alonzo, can your training section prepare, say, a light plane pilot to handle the rendezvous? Assume sixteen hours a day of hard work, and unlimited use of the RI Triple-trainer for the next three days.'

Alonzo Swain, the RI launch operations superintendent and a former astronaut, bowed his gray-haired head in thought. He lifted it to say, 'Possible, Hal, but highly doubtful. The controls aren't that complicated, but . . . there's a certain *feel* to operating under zero G, or three G's, that you only get through practice. I wouldn't send an aircraft pilot out there except as a last resort.'

'Just a minute, Hal. There's something I'd like to get clear in my head.' The speaker was Lambert Dawes, the company controller. He was a frail, thin wisp of a man, nearing retirement and not afraid of anyone, including Harold Hentson. 'If I've followed Raoul and Pete correctly, it will take eighteen hours of acceleration to match the Probe's velocity. You have a total fuel supply of twenty-two hours. How is the pilot—and the Probe, assuming he takes charge of it—supposed to get back to Earth?'

Harold nodded at Dawson, who again touched his fingers together and stared at them intently as he spoke. 'Lambert, assuming our pilot can disable the Probe's engines, in effect turning it into an inert body—Raoul and I estimate four hours of deceleration can throw it into a close pass around the sun. We can plot the angle of application in real time and try to guide it back to Earth. The second pass would be in about two weeks. At that time it would be necessary to meet it with probably one more Big Bird, and slow it enough to allow capture by Earth's gravity.'

Dawes looked astonished. 'But—if you're going close to the sun the heat inside will be tremendous! You can't build a shield against that in four days! This mission isn't dangerous—it's suicide!'

'Not necessarily,' Harold disagreed. 'The calculations aren't that firm. Three hours of deceleration may be enough. If so, the one hour you have left would be sufficient to move the Big Bird out to a safer distance. Remember, with most of its cargo of propellants gone it becomes a relatively light vehicle, while engine thrust remains the same.'

'That isn't much hope for a man you're asking to risk his life,' said Swain.

'There's also the unknown factor, Alonzo,' Harold went on. 'We don't really know what a man can accomplish until he's *there!* Possibly it will be nothing. It is also possible he may be able to get aboard the Probe, learn to fly it . . .'

Alonzo Swain nodded—But it was obvious he agreed with the fifty-six astronauts who felt the risk was too great.

'Hal, have you considered the legal aspects of attempting this mission?' The speaker was Fred Buck, the company counsel. 'Taking a rocket contracted to SB, and using it in an attempt to contravene a WorldGov decision, will bring down so much wrath on our heads the company may not survive. Are you quite sure you want to risk this?'

Harold looked around the table. 'Does anyone else have reservations, assuming we decide this mission is technically feasible?'

'Yes, I have a major one.' The only woman at the table rose to her feet. She was Maria Schnider, the employees representative. RI was forty-nine per cent owned by the people who worked for it. Maria was a production worker, but she attended every staff and board of directors meeting. 'I don't understand why we are even considering this idea. If WorldGov and Space Benefits don't believe we should interfere with the Probe, why is RI thinking of doing so? What can we possibly hope to gain that would make you willing to risk putting RI right out of business?

'Would you like to answer that one, Will?'

Wilhelm Wundt was the head of RI's small but highly competent Research Laboratory. On the organization chart Pepi Asturio worked for Wilhelm; actually his work was independent from that of the main group.

Wundt was a spare, gray-haired old man who moved in quick bird-like jerks and darts. His mind was diametrically opposed, being slow and deep. He had a broad, encompassing grasp across the whole spectrum of physics. He seldom spoke at staff meetings unless called upon.

'If you wish, Hal. Let me begin with what we know. MoonEye has furnished an estimate of the size of this strange craft. They calculate it at less than a hundred meters in length, half that of our largest cargo rocket. Such a small vehicle requires a power source far beyond anything we have today. It appears to use two phased pulse nuclear engines, each producing a relatively small thrust. These engines have been burning for three days now and will apparently continue to burn while it is in our solar system; first losing speed, then gaining it back. Spectroscopic analysis of the blue light reveals alpha particles and traces of nitrogen. It seems obvious its builders have mastered the technique of fusing a free alpha particle with nitrogen-15, which then fissions into four helium nuclei. This fusion-fission cycle produces thrust contained in a rocket nozzle. The amount can be precisely controlled. And of course a single kilogram of nitrogen yields a tremendous amount of energy, far more than we can obtain from equivalent deuterium-tritium fusion. As you know, nitrogen is plentiful and cheap. Also, the reaction is a very clean one, the even division of the nitrogen-16 nucleus into four helium-4 nuclei yielding very few radioactive by-products. Now as to why this produces such a huge blue flame—theory indicates it shouldn't. Further study is required.'

Wundt had plainly lost most of his audience. Harold repressed a grin and said, 'Suffice it to say that if we capture the Probe, the first application of new knowledge will be directly in RI's line of business. But that's just the start. This new source of cheap nuclear energy could revolutionize world power production. And what could we learn from the decision-making computer that is obviously directing the Probe? How much would it advance out studies in machine intelligence? What could we learn from understanding and using the ship's sensing instruments? Its analyzing machinery? It seems rather obvious that if we capture the Probe our patent licensing division will become the biggest money-maker we have!'

'What makes you think WorldGov would let us keep the Probe if we *did* the incredible and captured it?' asked Maria.

'They probably wouldn't,' Fred Buck suddenly spoke up. 'But if we took possession and filed a legal claim for salvage, we'd have an excellent case. I'm sure we could work out some compromise that would allow us first crack at the technology.'

A messenger entered the conference room and hurried to Peter Dawson's chair. The tracking VP scanned the note and stood up, suppressed excitement on his face. 'Good news! The Probe stopped its engines precisely ten radii from Jupiter. I believe you can now accept our projected flight path as a fact, not a postulate.'

Harold rose as Dawson sat down to a small buzz of conversation. 'Thank you, Pete; glad you had that confirmation rushed in here. I'll try to make the rest of this brief. I am convinced that if we succeed in capturing the Probe, Rockets International will benefit more than we can possibly imagine. And someone has to make the effort. If it's left up to WorldGov, a source of potential knowledge greater than any we have ever known will totally escape us. I think the project is well worth the financial risk to RI. As for the human life involved —the risks there are solely up to me, since I am going to be the pilot. We will proceed as outlined. Please return here again tomorrow morning with progress reports.'

Harold turned and walked out of the conference room.

Harold's office door had barely closed behind him when it opened again. Pepi, Alonzo, and Pete Dawson hurried in. Harold heaved an inner sigh and turned to confront the inevitable. These three were his personal friends as well as fellow employees. He could not simply tell them his decision was his business and send them on their way.

Alonzo spoke first. 'Hal, did I ever tell you I

think you're a goddamned idiot?'

'You're fired,' Harold said pleasantly.

'Kiss my ass. I can get another job. Now listen to me. There is no point whatever in you flying this mission. You couldn't handle the rendezvous when you got there. If you are dead set on this, if it absolutely must be done, then I'll go.'

'And how do I explain to Peggy and that brood of kids—five with the latest, isn't it?—what happened if you *don't* get back? No thanks, Al. If we can't get a qualified pilot, then the only person I'm willing to risk is myself. And why are you so sure I can't do it? I have almost four-hundred hours in light aircraft. You'll be here to guide me. And if the imprint works as well as Pepi expects, so will the first Jarl.'

'It won't work, Hal.' Pete Dawson's voice was calm but firm. 'Even assuming my boys could get you to the rendezvous point by ground control, you'd still have to do all the close maneuvering. At encounter we'll have a transmission time of several minutes. There is no way anyone here could help or advise you.'

'Then I'll train as intensively as I can for the next three days and manage without you,' Harold said cheerfully.

Dawson's face was somber. 'Hal—how much of this fanatical determination stems from the fact you always wanted to be an astronaut? Now don't bother to fire me—I just resigned, and I *will* speak my mind! We all know you flunked out of the Astronaut Academy because you couldn't handle the math. We know you worshipped your father because he was the first man on Mars, not because he served a term as President of the US. I ask you to examine your own motivations very carefully—and if you still think you are making a sensible decision, then I'll withdraw my objection.'

Pete Dawson's cool logic was utterly convincing, as always. Harold felt something inside himself shrivel and die. He had not actually explored his internal feelings after it became obvious the pilot was unlikely to return alive. Going himself had seemed the obvious thing to do. Now he realized it was a grandiose scheme, doomed to failure by his own inadequacies.

'There may be another way,' Pepi said into the sudden silence.

The other three men turned to stare at him. 'I know one highly experienced astronaut who would certainly volunteer,' Pepi went on. 'We can ask him Friday. Jarl Hentson should be fully with us by then.'

There was a moment of shocked quiet. An automatic *NO!* rose in Harold's throat; he choked it back. If the imprinting took as well as Pepi expected, if the extensive knowledge and pilot skills transferred over to the blank young mind . . . then sending Jarl might be the one workable solution open to them.

An image of young Jarl's face rose in Harold's mind. He loved his son, in the way one loves a helpless baby. Jarl had no intelligence, but he did possess some traces of personality, as his mother had pointed out. He was gentle, friendly, and dependent. But that which was cute and lovable in a baby seemed inappropriate in a husky nineteen year old.

Even assuming Pepi's confidence was justified, and the persona of the first Jarl agreed to go—could he really sacrifice his son this way? What kind of man was he, Harold Hentson, who could even contemplate such an act?

The answer, when it came, was from somewhere deep inside, springing from the very fiber and essence of his being. He had his own vision of what Mankind's goals should be, an older belief that went back to the last century. It was that Man had to keep striving, moving ever outward, or perish. It was more than the frontier spirit, above and beyond the need for challenge and growth. To stop was to degenerate.

Opposition to this point of view was plentiful. Since the first ecology movements of the 1960s, the first revolts against the philosophy of continual growth, a disbelief in science and technology had grown and swelled, to become a mighty force in the world. In 2011 every major technical advance was opposed by some group or other, with the result that many never went into effect.

Harold's particular interest in life was the space program. He had failed to become an astronaut despite his best efforts. Fate had then made him president of the world's largest aerospace company, rather than working directly for the government. And over the years, as familiarity bred a growing and deepening contempt for government bureaucracy, he had been glad it worked out that way.

Ultimately, any person acted according to his beliefs. And he believed with total sincerity it was vital to the future of Mankind that this Probe be captured and its secrets revealed. He would gladly keep that rendezvous in space himself, if he could make the mission a success. Since he could not, would he sacrifice his son—and with him, the persona of his father?

Harold looked deep inside himself, trembling on

the verge of a decision the consequences of which could hurt him for the rest of his life. If Jarl died—if that death came as a wasted effort—could Hal Hentson live with himself afterward?

That one he could answer. The thought of his son dying in a useless cause was unbearable, unacceptable—but if Jarl succeeded in this strange mission, returned the Probe to Earth and died a hero—that he could live with.

Harold could not clarify in his own mind why success or failure should ease or torment his conscience—but it would, and he had to accept that fact about himself.

But he had a little time yet in which to make the final decision. The imprinting might not be completely successful, and he would still need to go himself—a course much preferable to sending his son.

Harold broke the long silence. 'Gentlemen—and friends, if I may call you that on the job—we will move ahead full speed on the launch preparations. Alonzo, set up the triple-trainer for Jarl—but start a separate program for me, to be learned during the actual flight while ground control runs the ship. Believe me—one or the other of us is going!'

* * *

Thursday, June 9, 2011

Jarl awoke.

The first conscious sensation was of a steady, unrelenting pressure on his entire body. That heaviness was familiar, a known thing he had experienced before. His thoughts seemed to move like ants struggling in syrup, disordered and very slow, but after a moment he was able to identify the sensation—and with recognition came a mild shock. It was acceleration; and then he identified the muted thunder surrounding him, and the vibration. He was in a spaceship.

Jarl shook his head, feeling dizzy and suddenly sick. What was a man as old as himself doing on a spaceship? But the motion of his head had felt odd; easier to turn to the left than the right. And finally the subtle feel of extra pressure on his left side corrected his initial assumption. This was not true acceleration; he was in a flight simulator.

Which still made no sense. Why was a man who had served as President of the United States training for spaceflight? It was true he hadn't been an active astronaut for fifteen years, and needed retraining . . . No, there were younger men available for space exploration, whatever the mission. Why should he be preparing to ride a rocket again?

He was not only physically dizzy, his head seemed stuffed with pillows. He had felt like this a few times when he awoke with a severe hangover—alert but mentally crippled, unable to concentrate, thoughts drifting away when he tried to pin them down. It was a disturbing sensation, and the reason there had been only a few hangovers in his life. He had learned the fine art of drinking in moderation.

Jarl tilted his head and looked down at his body. He was dressed in a pressure suit and strapped into a pilot's couch of a new type he did not recognize. And with growing wonder, he realized he did not recognize the shape of his own legs, or the wide young hips above them, or the muscular hands that lay at his sides. He glanced around turning his head slowly to avoid heavy strain. He was in the pilot's cramped compartment of a two-man ship; or at least a simulation of one. The console in front of him looked reasonably familiar, as did the co-pilot's. But there was a shield in place over the lone window, as there always was when the giant simulator was in motion.

Jarl could almost guess where he was; in the fifty-meter triple-trainer at RI Plant 1. Building the three-arm centrifuge had been one of his last acts as president of Rockets International, before he resigned to run for President of the United States. He had been fond of telling his White House staff that the first presidency had been a much better job.

'Awake, sir? We would like you to eat, if you can keep the food down.'

The voice was from a small screen that had just lit up on the console. Jarl stared at the impassively polite face of a young man he knew at once had to be a flight controller. There was a cheerful and competent sameness about all of them that grew irritatingly familiar to a pilot.

It was difficult to assess his internal condition under a steady three G's, but Jarl tried. He noticed that his head seemed more clear, and he was having less difficulty concentrating on the business at hand. He said aloud, 'I think I can eat. And then I want you to tell me—'

'Good! One hot dinner coming right up. We'll answer your questions later, sir. Right now it's best you sleep some more as soon as you've finished.'

A moment later a tray of steaming hot food appeared in a slot at the bottom of the console. This was new; there hadn't been any facilities for food in the original three-trainers. But that had been a long time ago . . . how long? He was fifty-six years old.

Was that right? Was this really 2006?

The pillows were back inside his head, this time with the stuffing pouring out, totally clouding his thoughts. Jarl pulled out the tray and started eating. It was difficult under the steady drag of acceleration, but he managed. Why had this become a part of the training? No one stayed under acceleration so long that he had to eat. Even on the Mars trip . . .

The food was gone. Jarl saw a second slot for disposables and shoved the empty tray and plastic utensils inside.

'Very good, sir. And now we're going to put you to sleep again. Perhaps we can talk during your next wake period.'

'But I want to know—' Jarl began, then stopped, angry but helpless. The screen had gone blank. And it was only a short time before he started feeling drowsy again. At first he resisted, looking around for the needle they must have in him, ready to yank it out. But it was down somewhere in the pressure suit, hidden from sight and reach.

Jarl stopped fighting and relaxed, letting sleep take him. Over the years he had learned when to argue and when to bide his time.

4

Thursday, June 9, 2011

'Mr. Hentson, legally speaking I suppose that rocket is yours until we've signed the final buy-off papers. And I understand you are unloading the government cargo. But you are still contracted to deliver a space-tanker every month, and—'

'And we will,' Harold interrupted. 'We have the next two almost on the line.' It was best not to mention RI might use one of those two itself. 'The launch of that hunk of the Space Station won't be delayed more than two weeks, and you have enough H and O up there to last longer than that. I'll take the "late" penalty if SB chooses it.'

'How do you happen to know the amounts in the Station's propellant tanks?' demanded Harold's visitor.

Harold was both amused and angry. The pudgy, stuffy little man sitting across from his desk was Wardell Davis, the Space Benefits Agency Representative to RI Plant 1. Davis was one of those overly-careful bureaucrats who take such care never to perform a wrong action that decision-making becomes impossible for them. This one had been thrust into unwanted prominence because he happened to be the man on the spot when SB learned

RI was studying the possibility of intercepting the Probe.

'Mr. Davis, are you forgetting RI has the maintenance contract for the Space Station? That includes keeping the propellants section supplied with H and O. I receive a copy of the status report that goes to your HQ in Washington.'

'Oh. Yes . . . well—let's get back to the main point, Mr. Hentson. The SB administrator is very disturbed to hear you seem to be making some plans to, ah—go against the decision of the WP office to leave this strange spacecraft alone. We, ah . . . do not know the precise legal situation, but—'

'Nor do I.' Harold kept his voice even with an effort of will. It was late in the afternoon, and Davis was his last appointment. He wanted to be rid of the man and make a fast round of a few critical problem areas. 'We do know, though, that the Space Benefits Act of 2007 that upgraded NASA into an international agency also granted private companies the right to launch their own payloads. While SB may still be our largest customer, we have launch contracts with several other companies that are developing space manufacturing facilities. Since there is no known owner of this Probe, we consider claiming it a space salvage operation, which is perfectly legal and proper. Now what else is bothering you?'

'What else is *bothering* me!' Davis was openly sweating, and the fear on his face was genuine. 'Good Lord! Man, think what you're doing! What if that—that *thing* up there has weapons on it? Maybe it can defend itself, knock out any ship that comes near it. Possibly it could trace an attacker back to Earth! Didn't that occur to you? All the experts say we're its main target, that it must have picked up radio or holo broadcasts and aimed for us from the beginning. It's just using Jupiter as a free brake. Don't you realize that's why WorldGov decided to leave it alone, as soon as they were sure it was unmanned? If it wants to take readings on us as it goes by, let it! It'll be years and years before the message gets back to its owners anyway.'

'Did the Agency recommend to WorldGov that we not try to capture it?' Harold asked, his voice carefully neutral. He had no idea how much Davis knew about the decisions reached at SB HQ.

'I did get a little on that, on the scrambler circuit.' Davis glanced around and lowered his voice, though he knew every word spoken in Harold's office was recorded. 'Yes, when they checked into it and realized the best we could manage was a one-way trip, the administrator said to knock it out or let it pass. The public wouldn't stand for a suicide mission, even if we could find an astronaut crazy enough to go. And then I heard the final decision not to meet it with nukes was made by the WP himself! Yes, this went all the way to the top. The Premier of WorldGov, not some staff flunky, decided that if we couldn't capture it we'd just leave it alone!'

Davis was treading on dangerous ground; dangerous to the career he valued so highly. But the desire to seem important had overcome his usual caution. People like Davis proliferated in government service like bees swarming around an unguarded honeycomb. They were also the reason Space Benefits was almost entirely a contract-letting agency, with all the actual work done by private enterprise.

'That's very interesting, and I won't mention where I heard it,' Harold said. 'Thanks for coming by. Now if you'll excuse me, I have several things to attend to before I can go home.'

'Now wait a minute, Mr. Hentson, you haven't given me an answer! Are you going to call of the mission? What can I tell them at HQ?'

'Just tell them I'm busy communing with the spirit of my father,' Harold answered, rising. Pat Pajick appeared at Davis's elbow as if by quiet magic, summoned by a silent call.

Muttering and fuming, Davis let Pat escort him out.

Harold left his office by a rear door, descended to the ground, and followed a concrete walk to a one-story building directly behind RI Headquarters. This was Wilhelm Wundt's area, the RI Basic Science Laboratory. Harold nodded and smiled at several people who greeted him, most of whom he did not know by name. Inside he turned to the left, to an isolated wing. The human guard at the door waved him through without the formality of signing the register.

The second shift was already on duty, but Pepi was still hard at work. Harold found the plump Chilian overseeing the technicians performing the imprint operation. Jarl Hentson the Second sat strapped in a heavy chair, surrounded by a maze of machinery, a cap with thick attaching electrical cables on his head. His expression seemed peaceful and intelligent, possibly because he was unconscious.

'Where do we stand, Pepi?' asked Harold.

'It's going quite well,' Pepi answered with obvious satisfaction. 'The synapses seem to have accepted the new circuits without strain. We have him back in for a reinforcement, but this should be the last imprinting operation. We awoke Jarl while he was in the trainer an hour ago, and one of the flight controllers talked with him a little while I monitored. The persona seemed almost complete, just about ready to function. There was a—', he hesitated, looking troubled, '—a little something odd about the Jarl personality, as though . . . a hidden force was underneath and trying to push through. I can't describe it very accurately. But regardless, this final reinforcement should establish the persona so strongly it will last longer than the mission.'

'Am I right in thinking Jarl was the only astronaut to have his brain read?'

'I believe so. And they took his patterns because he went into politics and got elected President, not because he was the first man on Mars, or the guy who reorganized Rockets International and moved it to Florida.'

'I received a complaint from Engineering this morning that you have our largest computer tied up, and they want it. When can you release it?'

Pepi heaved an exasperated sigh. 'Hal, you can store the literally billions of circuits and patterns of an operating brain on tape, but you can't play them back one at a time. To create the persona you have to empty the banks in a very large computer and feed it all that data. Playing it back and imprinting the patterns on another brain is a simultaneous process, involving millions of currents moving at once. And even when we're through it isn't the complete original mind and can never be. But as I said, this is the last imprinting. Engineering can have its damn computer back tomorrow.'

'I'll check with you in the morning,' Harold said and then hurried off to the next critical area. That was Carson Jamison's office in Plant 1, just down the road from the RI Tower. He found the place empty; Jamison and his staff had gone home.

There was a lighted wall status board in Jamison's office. It changed just as Harold was reading it, the percentage of flight readiness jumping to seventy per cent. Jamison was easily beating his schedule. He'd have to remember to slide that man into a staff job somewhere, out of the main line of fire. There was no place in production for someone who was afraid to commit himself without a fat safety margin.

Harold leaned back in Jamison's chair, his eyes on the board but his mind elsewhere. A great many people were wondering why he had started RI on this dangerous and probably fruitless course. The odds against success were phenomenal. If even WorldGov had given up . . .

And Harold Hentson realized that was precisely what was driving him. He did not agree with the government's decision—and was one of the few people in the world in a position to do something about it.

He chuckled, thinking of what Jarl would say if he knew his persona was going to perform a dangerous job that would ultimately benefit WorldGov. The old man had hated the more powerful successor to the United Nations with a passion. He had stalled letting the US surrender part of its autonomy as long as he was President. The first major act his successor had signed in 2005 was the WorldGov membership agreement. A year later

Jarl had started the long process of feeding his total memory and all accessible brain patterns onto reels of tape. And in 2007 the supposedly sturdy heart had given out, and Jarl Hentson, first man to set foot on Mars, founding president of Rockets International, United States President 2001–2004, was dead.

Now the old man would soon be alive again, or at least his personality would. But he was to be secluded from all outside contacts except the flight controllers, with Pepi looking over their shoulders. No one knew how well-integrated the personality would be, and Pepi's staff had strongly recommended Jarl/Jarl be spared all possible shock. Harold would not even get to shake the hand of the man he had loved and worshipped more than anyone on Earth.

* * *

'So we have it confirmed,' said Jodie, looking around the small circle of people in the apartment. 'Jesus Hentson is going to defy WorldGov and try to capture the Probe, all by himself. Several of you who work at RI seem to think he actually has a chance, that if he sends his resurrected father the scheme might work. Which means we have to stop the launch. The next question is how. Suggestions?'

'Sure!' a heavily bearded young man named Sanderson responded. 'We can march on that rocket Sunday afternoon. They can't launch with about a thousand of us standing under the nozzles. I'm a guidance engineer for RI, and I can tell you it has to be launched during about a twenty-minute window. By the time they clear us out of the way, it'll be too late.'

'Will that work?' Jodie asked, looking around

the group. Several people nodded. RI was by far the largest company in the central Florida area, and many employees belonged to the various protest groups. Knowledge of their outside affiliations would have meant trouble with their employer—which only made most of them more determined to fight. It also furnished FOE and other protest organizations a cadre of technically trained people.

'We'll have to have boats,' Sanderson went on. 'Merritt Island can be easily assaulted over the Indian River, but not by land. Rounding up enough boats to ferry over a thousand people shouldn't be any problem.'

'Good. Then why don't you recruit enough help to form a committee and get started on preparations. Have the owners all in their boats with time to spare Sunday, get a signal set up, assign team leaders, and so on. But that's letting this thing run on till the last minute. Is there any way we can stop it earlier? What about the legal angle? Any lawyers here?'

'I'm an attorney,' a gray-haired man spoke up. 'Yes, there are several ways to mount a legal attack. But I can tell you that's already in process. I work for SB at Kennedy. The word buzzing the corridors this morning is that SB will go to court tomorrow for an injunction. It won't be served until Sunday, making it almost impossible for RI to counter before Monday—which will be too late.'

'Good! Strange though it seems to have SB on our side. Any other angle? Let's explore all alternatives.'

'I know one thing which would stop it,' said a very pretty olive-skinned girl with long black hair. She had been introduced earlier as Diana Sharp. 'I work at the Citizens National Bank of Cocoa Beach. And I know a way we can get directly to Hal Hentson, put him out of circulation until Monday. The launch won't go without him.'

'Oh? What's that?' Jodie asked.

The pretty girl looked uncomfortable. 'Sarcoma, I—can we talk alone? And I'll have to have your promise not to repeat this.'

Jodie rose and led the way into her bedroom. When the door closed the black-haired girl sat on the bed, looking at her feet as she talked. Jodie saw she was about twenty-five, with a somewhat lush figure, just tending towards plumpness. In a few years she would be fat and doughy-looking. 'Sarcoma, we have a—a special account for a Mr. Alexis D. Martin. The bank pays the bills on this apartment, the utilities, and so on, automatically. Making out the check is one of my jobs. He doesn't come into the bank very often, but he did once, about a year ago. And I—I thought I recognized him. It was just before quitting time on Friday, and my date was waiting for me outside. I got him to follow this Mr. Martin. He went to one of the local hot-spots, a pick-up place called the King of the Hill, and he eventually made contact with a girl there and took her back to his apartment for the night.'

'So?' asked Jodie, puzzled.

'Well—it was really Hal Hentson! He was wearing a dark wig and looked a lot different, but it was him. I've learned since he goes out almost every Friday night, usually to the same place. He always picks up a woman there and takes her back to that apartment, or to her place if she has one.'

The girl was obviously embarrassed, far more

than seemed warranted by the revelation Hal Hentson kept a private apartment for weekend pickups. Jodie leaned forward and placed a hand over Diana's, which were resting nervously in her lap. 'What's the matter, dear? What is it you aren't telling me?'

Diana raised dark eyes in which tears were shining. 'Oh Sarcoma, I—the very next Friday I put on a sexy split-waist dress, and went to the Hill, and I—I let him pick me up! And two or three times more over the past year, until he seemed to lose interest. He still speaks when he sees me, and he's very nice, but he won't take me if he can get someone new. And I've . . . I've been hiding this from my steady, who wants to contract with me for children, but wouldn't if he knew.'

'Well I'll be damned!'

Diana burst into tears, and Jodie hastily tried to comfort her. She took the sobbing form in her arms and rocked gently back and forth, petting and soothing her. The treatment was old but effective. Diana's sobs faded into sniffles. She sat up, reached for a tissue, and blew her nose.

'Do you think you're in love with the guy?' asked Jodie, keeping her voice soft and friendly.

'No; no, I'm sure I'm not. It was just a—a kind of cheap thrill, the thought I was actually in bed with the famous Hal Hentson. But he's like anyone else when you get to know him—you know? I'm telling you this because I thought you could use the info. But remember—no one is to know where you got it!'

'Of course,' Jodie said, patting her hands again. 'But you've given me an idea. I've been wanting to meet this egomaniac myself.'

Diana rose to her feet, a questioning look on her face. 'Sarcoma, you wouldn't—I don't want to see him hurt. He was always nice to me.

'Hurting people unnecessarily isn't our style,' Jodie assured her. 'But maybe we can just remove this great lover from the scene until Monday, after which it won't matter. Keep tomorrow night free. We'll need you to point him out for us.'

Diana nodded, and they returned to the main meeting.

* * *

Friday, June 10, 2011

Jarl awoke again.

He barely had his eyes open before the little screen on the console flashed on, and another smiling flight controller appeared. Their instruments must be very sensitive; probably had an electroencephalograph inside his helmet.

'Hello there! How about a little food, Jarl? Then we want to check you out on a few rendezvous techniques that may be new. Feel up to it?'

The thought of food suddenly made him amazingly hungry. Jarl nodded, and a hot dish promptly appeared in the slot.

Jarl ate as quickly as the constant drag permitted, moving his arms and hands as though working underwater. This young body was in excellent conditon—he clamped that thought off, tried to push it away. But below the cotton floating through his mind something stirred, and a vagrant thought came through. . . . *exercise* . . . *machines* . . . *arms up!* . . . *down!* . . . *up* . . . and then the intruding figment retreated into the fog.

Left behind was a strong feeling of love.

Jarl concentrated on the food. It was good; real, solid. His outside faculties seemed clear enough, despite the fluff in his head. He could worry about what he was doing here later. (And what *was* he? No. No, forget that one. Concentrate on the training. He had a mission to do, apparently an important one. The job first, always.)

Jarl finished the food and disposed of the tray. The image on the small screen watched him with quiet attention.

'And now I want some questions answered,' Jarl announced, his voice firm.

The young flight controller smiled. 'Okay, I'll try. But you may get tired again, so let's run through a few routines first. The rendezvous is going to be by visual contact, with you handling the maneuvering engines and attitude thrusters. We'll work the main drive from Mission Control, cutting off when you take over. We're going to be ahead of the target, which is accelerating at a constant rate. You'll do a 178–degree turn to the right, match velocity using the maneuvering engines, and let it come to you for the actual contact. Now the tricky part will be handling the thrust on the maneuvering engines. We want to spend a couple of hours running you through three or four different closing velocities. We'll feed the results into the flight computer and give you a readout on your main screen.'

Jarl felt a smouldering anger gathering in his throat. If they tried to put him back to sleep after the practice session . . . *but a soothing, calming sense of total trust welled up from somewhere deep inside, overriding the fear-based anger. They would take care of him. He had only to relax . . .*

Jarl shook his head in bafflement. Just when he seemed to be regaining all his senses, feeling able to respond almost normally, thoughts and attitudes alien to his experience were popping into his head. It was not in his nature to relax and expect others to look after him.

For the moment it seemed wisest to do as the controller asked. He obviously needed to practice for the upcoming mission. And until he knew more about this situation, he was in no position to make his own decisions.

Jarl went to work. It was a pleasure to flex old mental muscles, to find that in some ways his brain was as good as ever. The controls were improved models of the ones he had used in 1990 (how long ago was that?) on the trip to Mars. A little more sensitive and responsive, perhaps, but basically the same. He should have no problem regaining his old skills and doing his job—whatever *that* was!

Two hours later Jarl was tired but content. He finished a closing sequence, made an imaginary contact with the shiny-nosed vehicle boring through artistically dark space toward him, and relaxed.

'Very good!' the controller approved. 'You haven't lost much, Jarl, considering . . .' he stopped, looking embarrased.

'Yeah . . . considering!' Jarl felt a fresh surge of anger and resentment. His tiredness vanished under a spurt of adrenalin. He had never been a patient man. 'Now you tell me a few things, sonny. What is this mission I'm training for? And why me? I'm too old for spaceflight . . .' he stopped, not wanting to pursue that line. 'Look, trying to think something straight through is like wading in mud up to my butt! And I keep having funny thoughts, odd things that seem to pop out of nowhere and make no sense! I want to know what you've done to me!'

'Mr. President—Jarl—I'm only authorized to tell you certain things. Any information on matters other than the mission will come from your son, Mr. Harold Hentson; he'll talk to you later. Now as for the mission—this one is so important it makes pioneering landing on Mars look like a Boy Scout trip!' The young flight controller briefly explained the salient facts about the Probe. 'Your job, if the rendezvous is successful, is to get on board.'

Jarl shook his head in stunned amazement. So it had happened at last! A genuine extraterrestrial visitor was approaching. This was no flying saucer will-o'-the-wisp but an undeniably real star-traveler. He had always hoped this might happen in his lifetime, but . . . No; cut that one off.

The controller went on, 'Now the scientific brains at RI consider it unlikely the Probe will have manual controls. They also doubt if it will be possible for a human to understand an alien's programmer well enough to work with it. What they think you probably *can* do is disconnect the drive controls enough to stop the engines. The Probe will still have too much velocity to stay in our solar system. But you will have about four hours of main drive propellants left in the Big Bird. There will be an attach fitting on your ship's nose. You are to connect physically to the Probe and position per our directions. We will then perform a retrograde firing that will slow the Probe and force it into a tight orbit around the sun. Our best estimate is that we can throw it within about 20 million kilometers, and the velocity that remains will be enough to whip it around Old Sol almost in a U-curve. That should get you back here in less than three weeks. We'll meet our visitor with another Big Bird, and slow it enough to fall into Earth orbit.'

Jarl was silent, almost unable to believe what he had heard. The explanation sounded as unbelievable as some of the problems in engineering textbooks. Could it possibly be true? He looked around at the tiny pilot's compartment. It was quite real and solid. And there was no doubting he was in the flight simulator. The constant, demanding weight of three G's never faltered.

The flight controller was waiting, face preternaturally calm. Jarl said, 'That's the dumbest-sounding mission I've ever heard! Only an idiot would risk his life on it. If you're going within 20 million klicks of the sun, how are you going to insulate the ship? And how do you know that much heat won't damage the Probe? Your explanation is full of holes, Mister!'

The young face in the small screen grinned. 'Yes sir. Some of us think so, too. But those are our orders. And it *is* the only chance we have at all.'

Jarl noticed the younger man hadn't denied this was a suicide mission. And he was supposed to volunteer for it? Who the hell did they think he was! Jarl decided to save that area for later. He had some other urgent questions.

'Something else is bothering me. I was President of the United States for four years. I have the memory of fifty-six years of life. How have I become twenty again? I haven't had muscles like this for thirty years!'

The friendly smile on the small screen disappeared, and a veil seemed to fall over the guileless eyes. 'Sorry, sir; that's an area in which I'm not authorized to furnish answers. Mr. Hentson will supply those when he comes. Now the physio monitor here says his readings show you're becoming very tired. How about sleeping for a few more hours?'

Jarl Hentson looked steadily at the waiting face, until the younger man saw his anger. The reserved expression grew more pronounced. But the flight controller remained silent, and Jarl did not feel the expected sleepiness coming on.

'Okay! Let the sleep juice flow. But if that wild-hair son of mine is responsible for this, I've got a few things to say to him!'

The professionally calm face split into a wide grin. 'Yes sir. Maybe you can talk back to Hal. Not many of us at RI try it. See you in a little while, then.'

Two or three minutes later the drowsiness came and pulled Jarl under again.

5

Friday, June 10, 2011

'Hal, Fred Buck's staff just picked up a rumor Space Benefits is going to court for an injunction.'

Harold glanced up at Pat Pajick. 'On what grounds?'

'The rumor wasn't that specific. Most likely something very legal and abstract, such as interfering with the foreign policy of WorldGov—now that the US no longer has a separate foreign policy.'

'Is there such a thing as world foreign policy?'

'No, but that won't help us if they get the injunction.'

Harold glanced at the desk chronometer. Pat was right, as usual. In another hour most industrial and legal business in the country would come to a halt for the three-day weekend. It would be very difficult, if the injunction was issued, to file an appeal before Tuesday morning—and the launch was set for Sunday afternoon at 4:31.

Harold had half expected a move of this type. The fear on the face of Davis had been genuine—and there were billions like him in the world.

'And that isn't all,' Pat went on, smiling. 'The New Friends of the Earth, an ecology group very active here in Florida, held a meeting last night and announced this morning they were going to protest the launch. Volunteers have vowed to crawl up the rocket nozzles and block them with their bodies. The invasion of Merritt Island is set for Sunday afternoon.'

'Pat, what—in hell!—has ecology to do with intercepting the Probe?'

'This group is opposed to the entire space program and think of the Probe as just more of the same. They seem to be a bunch of extreme fanatics. The original Friends of the Earth was a good organization. They did a lot of hard work in preserving undeveloped lands and waterways, particularly in California and later here. I was a member myself for several years, until a bunch of die-hard fanatics took over and drove out all the people with the least bit of common sense. What you have left now is a bagful of mixed nuts.'

'Yes, I'm familiar with their recent activities.' Harold could recall several instances of protests in which FOE banners had prominently figured, usually those of important scientific launches to the other planets. 'But it still seems to me they are straying out of their field.'

Pat's smile had vanished. The discussion was drifting too much toward argument, in which he would not indulge. 'I'd better get back to work' he said quietly, and turned and left.

Harold stared at his assistant's retreating back. This lack of response was Pat's one weakness. Harold enjoyed bouncing ideas off other people and hearing their objections. He was capable of modifying his own views immediately if he learned something new and useful. Pat was not a 'yes' man, but neither would he press his own point of view.

But Harold had known that when he promoted Pat. You had to accept people as they were.

The Friends of the Earth were also one of the groups that had gotten the interstellar probe project killed last year. But they worked by whipping up public opinion, and that couldn't be done in time to stop Sunday's launch. Harold was more worried about the possible injunction. That was a real threat.

Harold checked through the stack of paper on his desk and his action pad. There was plenty to do, but all of it dealt with the normal operations of RI. Everything pertaining to intercepting the Probe had been done. And somehow he did not feel like tackling the more mundane work. The sense of driving urgency that had been pushing him all week was finally fading.

Harold called Carson Jamison and Goldstone for status reports, then went home a few minutes early.

The aircar was crowded—Harold wondered how many were RI employees getting an early start on the week-end—but he knew no one, nor did anyone start a conversation. At home he read for an hour, then caught the evening news. The media hadn't been tipped yet to the struggle between RI and SB.

Lily had prepared an excellent dinner. It seemed strange not to have Jarl with them, even though he normally ate with Robert and not at their table. Lily was preoccupied and silent throughout the meal, as she often was these days.

After dinner Lily curled up in front of the holovision, where she had probably spent most of the day. Harold went to his quarters, bathed, shaved, and dressed.

'Going out for poker?' Lily asked when he emerged.

The Friday night poker game was a pleasant fiction they both carefully maintained. 'Yes; don't wait up for me,' Harold said, and kissed her goodbye. Her acceptance of his Friday nights out was another reason they were still together.

It was a ten-minute flight to Cocoa Beach, but the aircar made several stops over the sixty-kilometer trip. Harold felt a gathering sense of excitement and anticipation. It was 8:00 when he finally reached the Royal Twin Towers in the heart of town. Harold got out and hurried to the service elevator. On the fifth floor he walked a familiar path, primarily through service corridors, until almost opposite his apartment. He met no one during the two minutes he was in the regular hallways.

Safely inside, Harold discarded his conservative gray suit and pulled a clinging, black, one-piece form-fitter from the bedroom closet. It had long sleeves and a wide collar that reached almost to the edge of his shoulders. In the back the collar hung down like a short cape. This was his favorite outfit, and he hadn't worn it in a month.

Harold pulled a clean jockstrap from the dresser drawer. It was mildly uncomfortable but mandatory in this costime. He redressed, pulled and adjusted the suit until it fit like a second skin and walked into the bathroom. He chose the very black, curly-haired wig from the four available and carefully pasted it on. It had short but bushy sideburns attached. Only a minute was required to touch-up his eyebrows until the color matched. Taking out his regular soft contact lenses, he substituted a pair that turned his dark gray eyes to dark brown. Finally he slipped on ankle-high boots of black vinyl and hung the strap of a small black purse over his shoulder. It contained credit cards, driver's license, and a social security card, all made out to Alexis Don Martin. The resemblance on all the photographs was close enough to pass.

Harold checked his appearance in the full-length mirror inside the bathroom door. There was a slight but noticeable bulge at the waistline; he needed to exercise more. Otherwise he still looked very trim for a man of forty-one.

The disguise would not fool a friend met at close quarters. But he did not expect to see any such tonight.

Harold removed some money and his car keys from a locked bureau drawer. At the door he looked carefully around, satisfying himself the place had a 'lived-in' look. There was only the living room, bedroom, bath, and a tiny kitchenette. A minimum of clutter made it seem occupied. Satisfied, he locked the door again and descended to the parking garage.

The steamer car was hard to start, a disadvantage of driving it only once a week. The flame finally ignited, and one minute later the 'ready' indicator said steam was available. Harold eased out into the heavy Friday night ground traffic.

Cocoa Beach, the island community which had been nicknamed 'Sin City' in the early days of space exploration, was still the liveliest area on the mid-Florida coast. The condominiums and towering apartment buildings that walled off the beach, almost from Jacksonville to Miami, were present here also. But on the inland side, along the beaches fronting the Indian and Banana Rivers, the density was not so great. Many one-story buildings and even private homes still survived.

Harold drove two kilometers north and turned west, on to the causeway leading to the mainland. At the edge of the Banana River he turned right, into the parking lot of a small, almost dark building. A discreetly lighted sign above the door identified it as the KING OF THE HILL.

He was a little early, and the place was less than half full. Harold waved to the pretty barmaid, whom he had dated in years past and took his usual place under Number 41. This was his private joke, that he shared with no one. He could pass for thirty-five and always gave that as his age.

Harold ordered his first drink, which the pretty barmaid knew to make rum-flavored and weak, and began the hunt.

When he had gradually realized Lily could never be a truly satisfying life partner, some fifteen years back, Harold had first gone the typical rich man's route of keeping a mistress. He had tried several and discovered to his surprise that compliant women and ready sex were not enough. He could only interact pleasurably with a woman who retained her independence, who was capable of saying 'No'—and could force him to earn her approval.

These Friday nights in another identity were also good for his mental equilibrium. Harold realized he was a strong personality and tended to dominate those over whom he held authority. Shedding the role of executive, putting his basic body and personality up front, compelled him to recognize his limitations. The arrogance that could grow in a man whom employees called by his first name, but most leaped to obey his slightest wish, was tamed, held down. He not infrequently would try for the most attractive sexob in the place—and lose, and return to the secret apartment to sleep alone.

Harold recognized that these failures were a necessary part of keeping in touch with the real world—but still competed vigorously to prevent them from happening.

He glanced around the long, narrow room. The band was on a dais at one end. the bar across the full width of the other. Every four-person table had a voice-only phone in its center and a matching number hanging overhead. There were even telephones and numbers at the bar.

It was just past 9:00, and the place was slowly filling. As usual, there were more men than women among the sexobs present. And a great many of the phones were already busy.

The three-man band began its first number, and several couples rose to dance. The open area in front of the bandstand was relatively small but could hold an astonishing number of bodies. Harold sat out the first two before getting a call from a girl he knew, Diana Sharp. They danced, and he learned Diana was there with a boyfriend—which was a relief, because he had no desire to become involved with her again. She had been fun for a few nights but had started dropping hints about contracting for marriage—obviously wanting to make their arrangement permanent. Instead, he had gradually broken off with her, though they remained friends.

Back at his table Harold saw that two new arrivals had seated themselves nearby. One was a short and very pretty brunette. Her companion was a tall and rather muscular blonde, wearing a permanently sullen and somewhat hostile expression.

Something about the two spelled 'lesbian', and Harold lost interest. But their phone rang, and the brunette answered. She evidently declined an invitation to dance. Over the next hour it rang several more times. About the fifth call she accepted the offer and danced with a slightly chubby young man barely taller than herself. After that she danced twice more, though the blonde never left the table.

That was atypical behavior for lezes. Harold continued to watch them as he danced several times, always with a woman he already knew. He struck out twice in trying for dances with attractive strangers. The pretty brunette continued to accept about one invitation out of five. He had no way of knowing if she knew the men or not.

At about 1:00 the crowd began to thin out. Harold had made passes at two of the women he knew but been turned down with pleasant smiles. The lovely brunette continued to intrigue him. Harold finally decided he had nothing to lose and dialed her number.

'Hello!' came the short woman's quick response.

'Hi! I'm Alexis Don Martin—Alex for short, at table 41. I notice you're very selective about whom you dance with. I hope I meet the qualifications, whatever they are. You're about the prettiest sexob in the room—though I think you already know that.'

As Harold was talking the girl's head turned until she saw him. She smiled but looked back at the phone to say, 'I decline anyone who tries obvious flattery, as you're doing.'

'Not so!' Harold said quickly. 'The truth isn't

flattery. That tall red-head in the gold skin-tights who was better-looking just left.'

The brunette laughed. 'You're either honest or quick. Go for the next one, then.'

It wasn't honesty that had caused Harold to respond that way. He didn't think the over-lush sex-ob he had mentioned was as attractive as this smaller woman.

In Harold's arms she stood about 155 centimeters tall, a good match for his own 178. The band was playing more and more slow numbers as the evening neared its end, and this one was a waltz. They moved through the gracefully formal steps with ease and pleasure.

'What can I call you?' Harold asked as she swung lightly on his arm.

'Jodie will do,' she murmured, eyes half-closed, a dreamy look on her face. Her voice was somewhat deep, throaty, and very appealing.

Jodie was dressed in a blue-velvet elastex body stocking that clung tightly to her figure, but did not outline every subtle curve and bulge like the stretchable skin-tights. Harold saw she was older than she had first appeared, approaching or past thirty. Her hair was as black as his wig but looked natural. She wore it straight and long, hanging below her shoulders. The nose was slightly snubbed, the large dark eyes framed by very long lashes. Her cheekbones were prominent, the lips short but full. There was a kittenish quality in the way she moved, in the warm smile that came quickly and lingered, in the husky laugh. But there was also an alert intelligence lurking around those lovely eyes, a certain cool aloofness.

Altogether, an intriguing woman.

Back at her table Harold thanked Jodie for the dance and returned to his own seat. To play the game by the rules he made another call, to a tiny Asian girl sitting at a table so close he could as easily have spoken direct. She accepted him for the next dance. The remaining sexobs, both male and female, were getting less discrimimating as available partners thinned out.

At his table again Harold called Jodie, who had danced with someone else, and was accepted for the next number.

'I just love the old dances,' Jodie said as they again moved through the easy grace of a waltz. 'Aren't you glad they keep bringing them back?'

'Yes, they're great,' Harold agreed. He would have agreed if she said the sky was falling. It was less than a half-hour before the King of the Hill would close.

'Would you like to join us for a drink?' Jodie asked when the music stopped. The kittenish quality was strong in her voice and smile.

Harold felt the first quick rush of blood, the heady feeling of triumph. 'If I can buy,' he said, still following formula.

'It's your money,' Jodie replied—an unusual response. At her table she introduced him to her friend, who went by the odd name of Strobe. They had three of what the women were drinking, which was Jupiter-Poos. It was an atrociously sweet concoction, but at least one based on his favorite alcohol, rum.

Some men were drifting out the door alone, having given up for the night. A few women were still at the tables, mostly middle-aged, ugly, or drunk. There was one more number, then the last drinks of the night, and the final slow dance to 'The Moons of Saturn', which Harold caught with Jodie.

When they returned to the table, Strobe had left. There was some money in front of her glass. Harold reached for their bill and the cash, and asked, 'Where did Strobe go?'

'Probably home. I told her you'd give me a lift, if she wanted to leave.'

'Oh.' Harold picked up his own bill, and paid both at the bar on the way out. This was becoming almost too easy, as though no further persuasion was necessary.

Harold unlocked his steamie and seated Jodie. Then he casually leaned inside and quickly kissed her, before walking around to the driver's side.

The burner caught immediately this time. During the sixty seconds of waiting he reached for Jodie. She obligingly leaned sideways, and their mouths met in a hard, passionate kiss.

The 'ready' indicator flashed on. When their lips parted Harold asked, 'Where to?'

'The Summerwell; I have an apartment there for the summer.'

'Then you don't live in Florida?'

'No; here on vacation. I'm a teacher in Minneapolis; high school.'

At the Summerwell, an older complex that rented to transients as well as local people, Harold parked in the number slot that Jodie indicated. Instead of getting out he reached for her again, but she stopped him with an upraised hand and a quizzical smile. 'Look, I picked you out of what was available; you don't have to work for it. Let's save the heavy stuff for later.'

Mentally, Harold shrugged; this little sexob

wasn't as ordinary as she appeared. Physically, he got out and opened her door.

Jodie led him into the front of the old building and up by elevator to the sixth floor. They walked down a long corridor to 618. She unlocked the door herself and ushered him inside. He stood blinking in the dimness when she closed the panel behind him. Then Jodie found the switch, and light flooded the room.

'Hi,' said the tall woman called Strobe. She was leaning lazily against the wall to Harold's right. One had held a pistol, pointed with casual competence at his stomach.

Harold felt his body tense from shock. That was followed immediately by a rising disgust. So it had all been a set-up, and his suspicion Jodie was proving too easy had been justified. But puzzlement replaced the suspicion. Why him? There had been a score of older and more affluent-appearing men in the Hill.

Jodie was smiling broadly. 'Come in, guys!' she called.

A bedroom door opened and three men filed out. Two were young, barely grown, with the straggling beards and matted hair that seemed the standard uniform of college freshmen. The third was older, about fifty.

'Slippers, get his keys and return the steamie to his regular parking slot under the Towers; you know the place. Jackie will be waiting for you with a ride back. Bill and Sergio, tie his hands.' It was Jodie speaking, but there was a subtle change in the husky voice. She spoke as someone accustomed to command, a quality Harold easily recognized.

The older man approached Harold from the side, keeping out of the line of fire. When he had the carkeys, Slippers left. The college students did a competent job of tying Harold's hands behind him. He watched intently for a chance to grab one and tumble him into Strobe, but they gave him no opportunity.

'We have a special room all ready for you, Jesus,' Jodie said, gesturing towards the bedroom where the three men had hidden. 'Behave yourself, and later we'll untie you.'

Harold felt a second shock. These people knew his true identity!

Jodie saw the surprise on his face and laughed, the husky voice tinged with mockery. 'That's right, Mr. Harold Hentson, president of Rockets International—we know who you are. And while we're taking off the disguises, I also have another name. The FacSheets call me—Sarcoma!'

The bewilderment Harold felt must have shown; he had never heard of her.

Jodie looked a little disappointed. 'Means nothing to you, I see. Well I'm famous in certain quarters, as you'll soon learn. Both the FBI and World-Gov Security have a thick file on that name. And it will be better known when we release you Monday, after it's too late to intercept that Probe.'

'But—sarcoma is a type of cancer!' Harold blurted as he stepped into the room. 'And why do *you* want to stop us from capturing the Probe?'

'Because the last thing this tired world needs is more space technology!' Jodie said and grasped the doorknob. As the panel swung toward her the short, full lips curved into a lovely smile, and the sexy voice sank to a low register. 'And you can think of *this* Sarcoma as a cancer in the connective tissues of Technological Man!'

The door closed, and Harold heard a lock click.

PART II

From the Master's Thesis scrapbook of Jarl Hentson

From an interview with Jacob Bronowski conducted by Science News editors Kendrick Frazier and Robert J. Trotter.

SCIENCE NEWS: . . . What about anti-science attitudes?

BRONOWSKI: Five years ago when the BBC and I started talking, one of the things that most moved me was when I was told by the senior BBC producer in charge of science programs as a whole that this might not be a good time to do these programs because the young people are in general anti-science. Well, I said, that's the first really persuasive thing that anybody has said to me. In that case I regard it as a duty to speak out about what I think to be the true philosophy of science.

SCIENCE NEWS: What do you say to those who would reject rational, logical thought?

BRONOWSKI: I recall one student group to which I was talking about the behavior of the big primates like the gorillas and how it was different from human behavior and why that had a great deal to teach us about our place in the world. And I remember one student saying, 'I know the chimpanzee has his bag, and I have mine, what else are you telling me?' And I said, 'Well, how do you know this?' and he said, 'I know it, I know it, I know it right here in my gut.' And I said, 'Well, the last person whom I remember telling us he knew it right there in his gut was Hitler, and incidentally he knew in his gut that you were a species of chimpanzee and not a species of Man.' (This happened to be a black student.) 'Now the reason we fought Hitler was that we thought the human species had other organs of sensibility than the gut. We know because we've really taken pains to try to find out. When I tell you about the chimpanzee and about Man, I may be wrong, but by God I've tried to be right, and that's more than could be said about you and Hitler.'

Science News
Vol. 104, No. 23
Dec. 8, 1973

6

Friday, June 10, 2011

The ceiling light was on. The first thing Harold saw was that all the walls had been lined with acoustic tile, thoroughly nailed down. The room contained an old-fashioned mattress-and-spring bed, a small table by its head, a dresser, and an easy chair. There was an adjoining bathroom, also with covered walls. There were no windows, but rectangular bulges in both rooms indicated areas where they had been boarded over before the tile was nailed on.

Harold inspected the bolts in the door hinges; they were welded in place. Someone had gone to a good deal of work to convert an ordinary bedroom into a cell.

It did not take Harold long to complete his inspection. There were several old FacSheets and books to read and an ancient built-in television set; evidently prisoners didn't rate Tri–D. Some kind soul had left a bowl of apples and oranges on the bedside table.

Having his hands tied behind him was uncomfortable. Harold resigned himself to the situation and lay on his side on the bed trying to think.

And with thought came fear.

Wednesday he had been ready to risk his life to capture the Probe, despite the high odds against success. He would still do so Sunday if necessary. But there was a vast difference between dying in action and having his throat slit like a pig in a slaughterhouse. The thought of seeing death approach, while he waited helpless, gave him the horrors.

Harold did not believe they would actually release him Monday. That statement had been a ploy to make him accept captivity quietly. It was safest for them to kill him after the launch had been stopped. Free, he would always be a danger to them.

The minutes dragged slowly past. Harold was too uncomfortable to sleep. As he lay in silence a second fear gradually overcame him, one he had not faced too often—the fear of failure. He wanted that rocket to rendezvous with the Probe. He had not felt so committed to a cause since his futile attempt to become an astronaut. In a way this intercept could be his redemption, his exculpation for that original failure. Surely capturing the Probe would be as important to the space program as the contribution of almost any astronaut.

If indeed it could be captured. If the attempt was made at all. If, in fact, he emerged from this room alive to confront his failure.

Harold lay on the bed for what seemed an endless time, worrying and fretting.

It was just after 4:00 when the door finally opened. He heard voices in the living room, but they faded when Jodie pushed the door closed. Evidently it was well sealed with weather stripping.

'Comfortable?' she asked pleasantly.

'I'd be more comfortable at home, thanks. And please untie me.'

'That I will do for you.' She crossed the room as Harold rose and turned around. 'Since you often stay gone on weekends, no one is going to miss you until near launch time Sunday,' Jodie added as she tugged on the knots. 'And without you there, we don't think your vice-presidents will have the guts to go ahead.'

The rope came off. Jodie tossed it to the floor and seated herself in the lone chair. She said, 'Sit on the bed and we'll talk a minute.'

Instead Harold took three steps and stood looking down into the very pretty face of his captor, rubbing his sore wrists. Jodie calmly returned the stare. 'Don't get any brilliant ideas about using force on me, Jesus. I'm a black belt and about twice as strong as I look. You're an office slug. I can take you in a fair fight.'

Jodie obviously believed what she said. And remembering their several dances and the lithe, easy way she moved, Harold could accept that she was in excellent physical condition. But the idea this small woman could whip a seventy-seven-kilogram man who religiously did his dull workouts in the health spa twice a week was silly. That was one of the many myths people who believed like the antitechs lived with.

But there were three men just outside the bedroom door, and probably Strobe and her pistol. This was not the time to attempt an escape.

Harold studied Jodie in silence. It seemed incredible that two hours ago they had been sharing a passionate kiss. He had hoped for a pleasant and relaxing night with this woman, knowing he would be working long hours over the weekend.

The damnable part of this was that she still seemed highly desirable. Her appeal had grown stronger; it should have diminished when he learned she was one of the antitech leaders.

A slow smile curved the full lips. Very quietly Jodie asked, 'Do I still look like a sexob to you, Mr. Harold Hentson?'

Harold turned away, still rubbing his wrists.

'I wanted to talk because I'd like to learn how your mind works,' Jodie went on, the voice much more friendly. 'I'd like to know why you are so convinced we need to capture the Probe.'

Harold shrugged. 'My reasons are obvious. That craft represents the next level in propulsion technology. If we can capture it whole, we can save twenty years and billions of dollars in development funds.' He told her in detail what the RI science staff had theorized about the Probe's fusion-fission reaction cycle, and possible applications.

Jodie nodded, her face very intent. 'Okay, so maybe we could use it to produce power on the ground. So what! Does having more power to burn make people happier? And do you really think more than a very few persons want to send astronauts or unmanned probes to other stars?'

'Probably not,' Harold had to agree.

'In the end, we grow old and we die. It's been that way a long long time. And all of your mighty science hasn't been able to add a year to the normal human lifespan. In the face of inevitable, unavoidable death—isn't it a crime to ask someone to devote his life to building something that won't bring him any direct benefits?'

'You're skipping blithely over the fact *most* people now live to be seventy or better,' Harold pointed out. 'It was once just a very small percentage. We owe that gain to science, which brought improved nutrition and medical care.'

'You miss my point. When life is so short, every individual should get as much out of his as he possibly can. How can you justify starting generations-long projects? Why should society make commitments that most of the individuals involved won't live to see completed?'

'Because Man is a social animal!' answered Harold, rising to pace the floor. 'We have to live and work together. Each and every one of us can have separate personal ambitions, but a society has to have goals that apply to all. Otherwise we fragment, we split apart into warring little segments, and ultimately into the final reduction, the individual alone. And a society can accomplish more for its members than any individual can possibly do for himself, no matter how hard he works.'

'But why *must* we "accomplish?" And who is to decide what?'

'The second question is easy. The leaders of the people—governmental, scientific, philosophical, religious—they decide what, as always. As for the need to accomplish—I think it's part of the basic nature of Man. How can there be a more definitive answer?'

'It's more nearly a basic tenet of Western civilization,' said Jodie, rising. She tapped on the door. It opened after a few seconds. Harold saw that one of the guards was standing in front of it but well away, holding the pistol. He was out of easy reach. And Harold would almost have bet a second man was standing against the wall, just out of sight. These people seemed very professional in their preparations, as though kidnapping was an old and accustomed tactic with them.

Jodie said good-night and walked out. The door closed smoothly behind her.

* * *

Saturday, June 11, 2011

This time Jarl awoke in bed.

His mind seemed foggy and dim. He could not tell if this was from sleepiness or the problem he seemed to have with his memory. After a time he awoke again, to realize he had fallen back asleep. He sat up to prevent further dozing, felt dizzy, and waited, upright, until that passed. Then he got slowly and carefully to his feet.

The disorientation was gone. He felt strong—and hungry again, as usual. He looked around the small room. It was a typical hospital set-up, with a dresser, adjustable bed, and adjoining bathroom. He used the latter, then searched for clothes. The dresser was filled with them; all were his size. (His *new* size? This time he tried to openly confront the strangeness, the wrongness—and discovered he simply did not know what to think. He did not have enough info. It would have to wait.)

Jarl shed his hospital gown and dressed in a dark blue two-piece outfit with a matching wide belt. He found some short black boots that fit nicely. He barely had them on when there was a knock on the door.

'Come in!' Jarl called, and a short, olive-skinned man of about forty entered. He was on the plump side, but moved with brisk energy. Jarl recognized Pepi Asturio.

'Pepi! By God, now maybe I'll get some answers! But first I want some breakfast and to stretch my legs a little. Where's the nearest food?'

Pepi grinned. 'Hello, Jarl. The company cafeteria is closed on Saturday, but I'll send out for breakfast. I'd rather you didn't leave the area yet, but we'll walk around a bit if you like.'

Jarl followed Pepi into a corridor and down it a short distance to an anteroom. A pretty young black girl in a nurse's uniform sat at the reception desk. Pepi asked her to have a breakfast sent in for Jarl, then led the way outside.

They were at the rear of a building Jarl recognized immediately. It was the RI Executive Tower. And the one where he had awakened was the Basic Science Laboratory. To his left, a half-kilometer away, was the massive bulk of RI Plant 1, where the astronaut flight training simulator was located. The buildings seemed little changed from the way he remembered them.

'What year is this, Pepi?' Jarl asked as they set off toward Plant 1.

It's 2011, Jarl. June 11, to be exact.'

'Then I've only been—gone—five years?'

Pepi hesitated. 'Well . . . actually just four. Your memories only go as far as the time your brain readings were taken, in 2006. You—lived—a year after that.'

'So I kicked off in 2007. And this—whatever I am—is that persona the physiologists took so long to make, the electronic re-creation of my functioning mind?'

'Jarl, we have a company psychologist who could probably put it in better words than I can. But I'm doing this because you know me, and we both felt that might make it easier for you. Frankly, we don't know just *what* you are! Instead of feeding the matrix patterns on the tapes into a computer, we imprinted them on the undeveloped brain of your grandson, Jarl the Second. Forcing a persona into an existing mind had been done experimentally, but only with persons dying of incurable diseases, congenital idiots, and so on. You're the first case of which we know where the imprint was performed on a direct linear descendent. It seems to have been an almost complete transfer; possibly because young Jarl's brain was virtually a blank slate.'

'No, not quite,' Jarl corrected. They were moving through the bright sunlight of a typical Florida spring day, over concrete sidewalks bordered with narrow flowerbeds. The side entrance into the towering south wall of Plant 1 was just ahead. 'I'm sharing this brain with whatever was already there. I keep getting odd thoughts, little bits and pieces that make no sense. And I also get a lot of emotional feeling, things that don't seem to be expressed in words but are very real.'

Pepi nodded. 'It figures; a good deal of the original personality must have survived. We all have emotions, and the brain reading wasn't really designed to pick them up. I think the working mental processes are mostly yours, though, because those patterns in young Jarl were very weak and undeveloped. You'll be mostly Jarl Hentson the First while the imprinting . . . lasts.'

The words jarred Jarl. Pepi swung abruptly to the right, on a walk that bordered the south side of the giant building. They passed a sharp-eyed guard, who gave Jarl an inquiring look. He was not wearing identification. Pepi flashed his own badge, which carried the red stripe of management across the top, and motioned for her to continue on her rounds.

'Pepi, I think you'd better explain that last remark *in detail!*'

'I will—but I wish to hell Hal was here to do it!' Pepi said unhappily.

'And just where *is* my wild-hair son?'

'Nobody knows. He was expected in this morning but didn't show. I called Lily. She said he went out as usual last night for a poker game and isn't back yet. She also said not to worry, that he often didn't return until Saturday or Sunday. Which might be true under normal circumstances but not when we're trying to get a launch off tomorrow. I'm afraid something has happened to Hal.'

'One problem at a time. First, what was that again about "while the imprint lasts"?'

Pepi grinned. 'Jarl, you seem about as clear-headed as the older man I remember. Okay, then. When we pour a persona back into the computer and establish the matrices, they last as long as we keep power to 'em. But the power potential in the human brain is infinitesimally low by comparison. Theory predicts the imprint should start fading in about two weeks, be completely gone in three. This brain and body should return to what they were, unless there are residual changes brought on by the unusual cortical activity. There, I've said it! And I hope to God my common sense is better than the psychologist's professional opinion. He thinks you shouldn't be told.'

They had reached the end of the building and the sidewalk inside the fence that paralleled the highway. Pepi turned back toward the RI Tower. 'Your breakfast should be there by now,' he said conversationally. 'How hard is all this hitting you?'

'Pretty strongly,' Jarl admitted. 'But I'll survive. Okay, I'm an electronic persona imprinted on the brain of my grandson, who was born an idiot. I won't be here but two weeks as a fully functioning mind. And during that time I'm supposed to pilot one of RI's Big Birds—which you've obviously rigged for maximum velocity rather than high load capacity—and intercept this Probe from some other civilization. This is a suicide mission for me, but if I succeed, Earth will capture our visitor. Is that the situation?'

'Precisely!' said Pepi, his voice low. He sounded worried.

'And I don't need to be told who dreamed this up,' Jarl said grimly. 'Only Wild-Hair Harold could think of anything so preposterous. How the hell has he kept RI from going broke since I made him president?'

'RI is doing very well. We're still by far the largest contractor in the space field. Better than half the Space Benefits budget goes to us every year.' He saw Jarl's puzzled look and added, 'The old National Aeronautics and Space Administration went international and became the Space Benefits Agency two years after the US joined WorldGov.'

Pepi saw Jarl's frown and shook his head, laughing. 'Damn, there I go again! Knowing how much you hated WorldGov, it was suggested you not be told we really work for them now. Sorry, Jarl; maybe it *would* have been better for you to get this background from the psychologist.'

'Pepi, there's so much I'm behind on. And I doubt I'll get caught up in two weeks. The world seems to be changing as fast as ever. Answer me one quick side question, though. That coalition of antitechnologists, environmentalists, and one-worlders who defeated me for re-election in 2004—are they still a potent force in the US?'

'The one-world movement died away when the US and China joined WorldGov. There was nothing left to fight for. But the environmentalists are still here, and stronger than ever. Their green-belt program to preserve the eastern woodlands is succeeding nicely. Some of the fringe elements operate outside the law, but most are legitimate.'

The two strolling men had reached the front entrance of the Tower. They walked inside, past a gray-haired old man in a guard's uniform standing just inside the door, through the lobby and out the rear to the laboratory. Jarl's breakfast was waiting in his room.

Pepi was silent while Jarl ate. When he finished, Jarl pushed the tray away with a contented sigh. 'Damn, I'd forgotten how good it is just to have an appetite and satisfy it. All my memories are of not caring any longer about food. This body makes a liar out of them.'

Pepi nodded. 'We expected a great many such conflicts, Jarl. But you seem to be overriding them very nicely. I think the imprinting, and hence your original personality, are strong because the brain is genetically very similar to your own. All three Hentsons could pass for fraternal triplets, allowing for different ages.'

The two men separated for a few minutes while Jarl went into the bathroom and brushed his teeth. This was one of his peculiarities. The fact that he could not clean his teeth immediately after formal banquets had always bothered him. Pepi was waiting in the reception area when he finished.

'Jarl, one of the several reasons I wanted to talk with you was that we have some complications due to Hal's absence. Fred Buck—I'm sure you remember him—thinks we should get a signed permission form from you before liftoff. It will say something to the effect you are really the original Jarl Hentson and fully in control of this body and mind. That you are voluntarily entering on a mission of which you understand the danger and are going so for the benefit of Mankind—blah blah and etcetera. This is to protect Hal in case of later repercussions.'

'I've got two weeks to be fully alive. Two weeks, and then I start fading back into nothingness. Hasn't it occurred to you—and to Wild-Hair, and the psychologist, and all the rest—that I may not *want* to spend that time dying on some impossible mission for the improbable good of Mankind?'

'Sure!' Pepi answered promptly. 'But we expect you to accept *because* you won't be here but for two weeks—and because Hal is determined to go if you don't. We couldn't find an experienced astronaut who would volunteer.'

'Hal? He couldn't handle a space rendezvous! He'd foul it up and kill himself besides. Where's the paper? I'll sign.'

'The thought that you'd refuse was never taken seriously,' Pepi said, rising. 'And everyone agrees with you Hal would be sacrificing his life for nothing. I'll get the form and two witnesses.'

Jarl watched him leave. And somewhere in the remote depths of the guts that fed the healthy body of Jarl Hentson the Second a tiny voice was crying, in a communication without words—*Oh let me live! I don't want to die!*

Jarl ignored the inner voice. His grandson's body was going to be sacrificed in the greatest adventure offered to a man since Armstrong and Aldrin walked on the moon. With that it would have to be content.

7

Saturday, June 11, 2011

'FRIENDS OF THE EARTH! Welcome to the rally! It's good to see so many of you still care what happens to this wrinkled old apple we live on.'

Strobe was serving as warm-up speaker, using a hand-held amplifier. She walked back and forth on the small platform, facing the crowd gathering on the grass. To her back was the little round lake some wag had named Lorna Doone, the main attraction of this small park in downtown Orlando. Across Church Street to the east was Tinker Field, where a new and larger Tangerine Bowl had recently been completed.

'We called you down here this lovely Saturday afternoon because we may have a job to do!' Strobe's amplified voice rolled on. 'I see people here from Daytona, from Melbourne, from Kissimmee, from Sanford. Know that you come in a good cause. Once again, our bodies may be needed on the firing line. Once again, we must be ready to do our share, make our contribution. And to tell you about that job, and what we may need of you, I'd like to introduce a very special guest. She came down from Boston just to be with us for this battle. Friends of the Earth, let me introduce a frequent contributor to the Bulletin, a member of the FOE national board of directors, and a fighter even more famous under another name—which we won't mention aloud. I give you Jodie Carson!'

Jodie rose from where she had been sitting in the front row and mounted the five steps to the platform. Strobe surrendered the amplifier and took a seat.

There was a polite burst of applause, which swiftly grew louder when word passed through the seated ranks that this was actually Sarcoma. Jodie held a finger over the mike button and waited, feeling her breath come faster. She was always nervous before a speech. The feeling faded rapidly once she started talking.

'Friends, first let me thank you for showing up today. We had hoped you wouldn't be needed, that Rockets International would have the good sense to call off their mad plan of trying to capture the interstellar Probe. But the latest word we have, as of about noon, is that the company officials in charge are still preparing to launch tomorrow. This in spite of the fact Jesus Hentson is missing, and has been since last night. He seems to have . . . er—disappeared. At least he can't be found.' Jodie waited for the implication to sink in and joined in the heavy laugh that followed.

'Friends, we are still hoping it will not be necessary to take any action. Strange though it may seem, WorldGov, through its Space Benefits Agency, has for once made the right decision. Namely, that they will not attempt to interfere with the Probe in any way and will even obtain injunctions to prevent private parties from doing so.' Jodie paused, but continued pacing back and forth on the narrow edge of the platform. She felt alive, vibrant with energy, strong and capable. She lived for these moments of high-voltage excitement, the response and support of a crowd. Only when she was actually leading a charge against some steel bastion of technology did life reach a higher peak, seem more fulfilling and worthwhile.

'What we are asking today is that you leave your name and visiphone number with our co-ordinating committee. The launch is set for 4:31 p.m. tomorrow. We will know before noon if they still intend to go through with it. If so, the word will go out to meet at the Riverside Park north of Titusville. We will have over a hundred boats, which will take most of us across the Indian River to Merritt Island. Then it's just a short walk across the sand to the launch site. We won't be able to get inside the pad fence and actually crawl up the rocket nozzles, as some have suggested—' she waited for the laugh to subside '—but that won't really be necessary. If they were to launch that giant vehicle with us jammed around the fence, I understand the concussion would kill us all. And I don't think even RI will have quite the nerve to wipe out a thousand of us!'

'You don't know Hal Hentson!' a voice called from the crowd.

Jodie lowered the amplifier and laughed. She raised it again to say, 'I've met the Son-of-God-Hentson!' And in a low and confidential voice: *'Just call me Hal, folks, just call me Hal!'*

When the expected laugh died away Jodie went on, 'You can call him anything, but just don't get in his way! Now I imagine some of you work for RI. You can't be fired for freely expressing your opinion in a protest, but your name could get on that confidential and highly illegal blacklist they maintain up in the RI Tower. So we're suggesting all RI employees wait at the beach, or in the boats. Don't go into the areas where you might be arrested. As for those of us who will be at the fence, we'll do the usual thing when they pull us away. Go peacefully, but walk back the instant the security guard lets go of you, if you can, and take up a new position. Remember, we only have to delay this one a half-hour and it's all over. And they can't haul that many of us away that fast!'

There was a small burst of applause. Most of these people had been arrested at one time or another. Jodie, looking over the crowd, was surprised to see how many middle-aged and even elderly persons were present. The Orlando chapter was an old one. The group that had originally saved the Everglades in the 1980s had broken up, but many members belonged to the new FOE. And some of these gray-haired retirees were the same dedicated young people who had fought that old battle to a successful finish.

Jodie lifted the amplifier again. 'While the various area leaders are taking your names and visiphone numbers, we have a very fine group to perform for us. Thank you again for coming, and I hope I *won't* see most of you tomorrow, because there will be no need. Now here's our Orlando chairperson to introduce the entertainment.'

Jodie surrendered the amplifier to a vigorous and ruddy-faced man who must have been approaching eighty years in age. Behind him, a group of four were setting up their instruments. Jodie nodded and smiled at several people who rushed up to shake hands or remind her of past acquaintance. She gradually worked her way to the edge of the crowd, joking and chatting as she went, but never stopping. Strobe appeared by her side, then Cindy and Inez. They reached the sidewalk and left the last of the FOE members behind as they hurried to Cindy's steamie.

'I think our second line of defense is in good shape,' Jodie said with satisfaction as Cindy pulled out into the heavy Orlando traffic. She had a sudden thought and laughed aloud. 'You know, I wish we had a recorder going in the RI conference room right now! Without Jesus there to tell them what to do I'll bet the RI Big Pigs are having one hell of a hot fight!'

The other three joined in her laughter. When it died away, Cindy said, 'I wonder which one of them had the nerve to keep the launch preparations moving.'

* * *

It had been Carson Jamison.

Carson was also presiding over the impromptu meeting he had called in his own conference room at Plant 1. Pepi Asturio, Raoul Stone, Peter Dawson, Alonzo Swain and Fred Buck were present.

'Gentlemen, I somewhat hastily asked you here because I haven't heard a word from Hal since yesterday, and he can't be located. The preparations for the launch tomorrow are going smoothly, and Alonzo tells me we won't have any difficulty meeting our schedule. But the big question is—what do we do if Hal still isn't back by then? Has he made a definite decision to send young Jarl? If so, do we want to launch his son without him being there?'

Carson was being his usual cautious self,

thought Pepi. He had received his orders and even in Hal's absence had faithfully carried them out. But it had been momentum alone that had gotten him this far. Now that new decisions had to be made, Carson wanted others to share the responsibility.

'Carson, aren't you starting to worry prematurely?' Pepi asked. 'We all know Hal has a habit of disappearing over weekends. Why not wait until tomorrow afternoon before making the final decision?'

'Because it's going to cost us a small fortune!' Carson nodded at his launch superintendent. 'Alonzo tells me we have over two hundred people working today. It will take that many or more tomorrow for the launch. And I'm having to charge all this against administrative expenses. It's throwing my budget completely out of whack! If we call this thing off now and cancel the second shift coming in, we can save RI a hundred thousand dollars. Plus the thirty million represented by the vehicle.'

'Plus get us back in the good graces of SB. Plus make our contract requirements on deliveries of Big Birds. Plus maybe save RI from making a fool of itself as a corporation, and going out of business when SB cancels all our contracts!' The speaker was Fred Buck, who up till then had been silent.

'But what if Hal *does* get back tomorrow and finds we can't launch because you stopped preparations?' Peter Dawson asked Carson.

'It would cost me my ass,' Carson said, his voice low. 'I still think we should stop it—but I'm not willing to make that decision alone. That's why I asked you here.'

'For your information, gentlemen, I've just had

our attainable velocity calculations rechecked,' Raoul Stone spoke up. 'Based on the 6:00 a.m. data from Pete's boys at Goldstone, the Probe is right on schedule. We can definitely intercept that fellow if we want to.'

'And what happens if you *do* get next to it?' asked Alonzo Swain.

Raoul grinned. 'Good question. Who the hell can say. The probability analysis worked up by Wundt's bright people says the Probe won't be armed. But they think like you and I, no matter what ratings they took in physics. The people who built that thing may not.'

'Carson, if you called us here because you want our opinions, I'll give you mine,' Pepi said into a brief silence. 'I think we should proceed full-speed ahead on the preparations and not make the final decision until just before launch tomorrow. If we still haven't found Hal by then—and I'm very much afraid something has happened to him and am going to ask Lily to file a missing person report —we can always stop it at the last minute. That will save the major expense, the vehicle itself. But if we cost RI the chance to capture that Probe just to save a hundred-thousand—well, I don't think Hal would forgive us for that. I strongly urge we continue the project just as he laid it out for us: at least up to launch time.

'I concur,' said Peter Dawson immediately.

'That certainly sounds like the safe and sensible thing to do,' said Carson, sounding relieved. 'Does anyone disagree with that assessment, or have a different recommendation?'

'I think it will be an exercise in futility,' said Fred Buck. 'SB is going to serve that injunction on us, and I will strongly advise RI not to defy it. But we can go ahead at present, yes.'

'Before we break up—Pepi, how's young Jarl?' asked Carson. 'I've thought all along this was the weakest part of Hal's plan. Do you really think a retarded boy like young Jarl could have learned enough from your treatment to be a better astronaut than a plane pilot?'

The way the question was phrased indicated Carson did not understand what had been done with Jarl the Second's brain. 'Carson, the imprinting has been successful beyond our highest expectations. For the next two weeks that's really old Jarl Hentson back with us, and as ornery as ever. Jarl is certainly capable of maneuvering the craft through the contact routine. The tough part will be getting inside and shutting off the Probe's engines. And we won't know what Jarl, or anyone else, can do in that area until we try.'

'But it's still a suicide mission,' pointed out Peter Dawson. 'We'll have to turn off the life support to keep Jarl from frying alive when he passes around the sun.'

There was a brief silence. Then someone softly said, *'Jesus!'*

* * *

Harold had slept late and been awakened at noon for a sandwich and some hot coffee. It was quiet in the small bedroom. He tried to read after eating but dozed off again. And then faint sounds of music reached him, and he shook himself awake and crossed to the shielded door. With one ear against the panel he could hear both male and female voices. Some of their friends had brought his captors a stereo, and they were playing it—loudly.

Which gave Harold an idea.

He walked into the bathroom and carefully examined the area where the window had been boarded over. With a set of carpenter's tools it would be possible to rip off the acoustic paneling . . . but there was no telling what lay underneath. And outside was a six-floor drop to the sand of Cocoa Beach.

Still, this seemed his best chance. Opening that locked door to the living room, and overpowering alert guards, was virtually impossible. What he needed was a good crowbar . . .

Harold walked back to the bedroom. There was only the bed, the television set, the chair, the table, and the dresser. The chair was a reasonably modern air-bag inflatable, but the other furniture was very old.

Harold stepped to the bed and lifted the coverlet. He was starring at a metal rail that ran the full length of the bed, its ends fitted into slots in both footboard and headboard.

Harold felt his breath come faster. He started to yank the rail out of the footboard, then changed his mind and hurried around to the side next to the wall. After a moment of beating down on the footboard with the palm of his hand, he managed to free the rail. The front end was more difficult because he had to support the mattress and springs, but he finally freed it also.

That side of the bed fell to the floor. Harold was holding a piece of thin metal angle iron longer than himself. From each end double attaching hooks protruded, fastened to shorter pieces of angle iron riveted at a 90 degree angle to the length.

Except for the fact the rail was too long and awkward, he had a fair crowbar. Harold lowered one end to the floor, placed a foot in the center, and bent the rail until the two ends were less than a meter apart.

Now each end could serve equally well. Better and better. Harold thought a moment, then turned on the television. He found a station playing mostly canned music over a silent newscast and turned the volume on loud. Then he went inside the bathroom and closed and locked the door.

Picking a spot where two tiles joined, Harold worked an edge of the angle iron underneath one side. Then he pulled, hesitated when the steel started to bend, shifted position, and pulled again.

A nail creaked and moved. Very slowly Harold started working the thin metal down the length of the tile. The next nail screeched and almost popped out.

It was awkward, clumsy labor. Sweat popped out on his forehead. Some nails did not want to pull free, and had to be pried at again and again. But little by little he was stripping off the concealing layer of tile.

Harold glanced at his watch, and saw to his surprise it was almost 6:00. They would be bringing his dinner in at any minute.

Unlocking the bathroom door, Harold hurried back into the bedroom. The first thing he saw was the mattress and springs, lying with one side on the floor. Hastily he gathered up the several books they had thoughtfully provided him and stacked them under the springs. By turning the last three upright he managed to raise the bedding high enough to seem normal. Pushed back against the wall, it would pass.

Returning to the bathroom, Harold bathed his

face and hands. He had barely seated himself in the chair and started watching TV when the door opened and Jodie entered, carrying a tray of food.

'How's the prisoner of humanity?' Jodie asked, setting his food on the bedside table.

'Starving,' Harold replied, getting hastily to his feet. 'Here, you take the chair and let me eat.' She had started to sit on the edge of the bed. He turned off the TV as he went by. Harold noticed Jodie watched him carefully as they passed within a meter of each other.

Harold seated himself carefully, trying not to be obvious about it. She was alert for trickery—but of the wrong kind.

The hard work had given Harold a real appetite. He ate hurriedly, as Jodie idly watched. This time he had a full take-out dinner. When the last scrap was gone she said, 'One more day and you can go home. By this time tomorrow there'll be nothing you can do.'

'I can try to put you and your gang in jail.'

'None of us have used any names except special ones known just to each other. You'll never find us. I'm the only one with a record, and it's only as Sarcoma. If we thought you really *could* identify us I'd be arranging now to have you shot.'

'Would you really? Are you so convinced of the righteousness of your case you'd even kill for it?'

'I've never killed anyone, but I would if it was necessary. For people like you, there's a special little group that does that kind of execution, some sky-high types who enjoy it. They aren't members of my organization, and we ask them for help only when nothing else will win the battle. And as for the morality of killing, which seems to horrify you

—have you ever thought of the millions you and all the other Big Pigs like you are quietly killing every year?'

'N-o-o,' said Harold slowly. 'In fact I wasn't aware I was killing anyone.'

'That's because you and the rest of the so-called leaders of the world don't see the consequences of your actions. If a new baby dies in Algeria because it needs a blood exchange at birth, you don't accept blame for the fact there's no hospital available. If a middle-aged man in Brasilia dies of a heart attack because he lives on a high-starch diet of corn and bread, you don't blame yourself for the fact he had no protein. But the billions the US and then WorldGov have wasted developing big rockets and assembling that useless space station would have built a thousand hospitals, and provided meat to millions of hungry people. But you don't *see* them! They live their miserable lives, they die their miserable deaths—and you and all the rest of the Big Pigs live fat and happy at the world's expense! That's why I hate your kind, *Jesus* Hentson! You kill every day—and you don't even know it!'

For the first time since Harold had met this strange woman she seemed to have gotten genuinely emotional. There was a wet shine in her eyes, and high color in her face. She was even breathing deeply, as though in the grip of some compelling passion.

A sudden insight dawned, and Harold started to speak. He choked it off. It was that this woman was one of those people who always fail in person-to-person relationships, who have no true friends and few close acquaintances. They really didn't like other people at all, but hid this from themselves by proclaiming their love for humanity as a whole. In short, this was one of the basic personality traits of most of the world's leaders!

'When you die you want it to be gloriously, in a mighty battle for something you believe in,' Harold said softly.

Jodie looked startled. 'That's very astute,' she admitted. 'I don't know how it relates, but—it's true I can't see myself dying in bed of old age . . . Okay, you reached me. But you hit me on a personal basis, on what I, Sarcoma, am.' *He noted with interest that she thought of herself as the glamorous outlaw Sarcoma—not Jodie.* 'Now get back to basics. Do you deny that the space program deprives poor people of a better chance for a decent life here on Earth?'

'Yes I certainly do! The space program is the cutting edge of new technology and has been now for fifty years! Those hospitals you mentioned have hundreds of new tools and techniques, from body sensors to cryogenic scalpels, developed first for space applications. That hungry old man has his crops guarded by satellites that warn his government immediately if a blight appears, or even if they get too dry and start dying.' Harold paused, studying Jodie's face. It was still filled with lurking fire. 'Look, we could argue all day and not get anywhere. Why don't you shed your clothes and hop into this bed, and we'll settle this man-to-woman.'

'My God! You're really cruddy-crude!'

Harold gave her a mocking grin.

'Oh I see,' Jodie said, her voice very quiet. 'You think I'm a lez, and you can hurt me by saying that. Sorry to disappoint you. *Jesus.* I'm hetero—despite the fact you find me with Strobe and Slippers. But

I'm particular whom I share it with—and you'll never make the grade!'

Jodie rose and walked out.

Which was what Harold wanted. He had to get back to work on that window.

8

Saturday, June 11, 2011

Harold relaxed, for the first time since Jodie entered the room. For a moment he had thought he misjudged her, that she was about to accept his dare—which would have brought down the bed and his own fragile chance of escape.

Nor had he really thought she was a lesbian. But the coarseness of his proposal had been an effective way of getting her to leave.

He turned the TV back on, locked the bathroom door, and resumed prying on the slowly yielding tiles. Already he could see the ends of two of the boards that had been nailed across the window.

It was midnight by the time he had access to the ends of three of the boards. They were of much heavier stock than the tile, and the nails more deeply driven. But whoever had done this work had been a poor carpenter. He had cut the boards so short barely three centimeters extended past the nailheads. By hammering gently with the edge of one of the attaching hooks on the rail, he managed to split one board end down to the nail. After that he widened and deepened the crack, and eventually worked one edge of the board up past the nail.

Harold ripped a long section loose with his bare hands.

With room to get the whole end of the bar between two boards and pry, the rest was easy.

There was no time to loosen the board ends still under tile on the opposite side. Instead Harold pulled the two free bottom ends down and a third one up, until he had room to crawl through. He found the small lever that operated the window and opened it. After that he had only to punch his way through a fragile plastic screen.

With his head and shoulders through the hole, Harold looked around. He was facing the ocean one hundred meters away—and it was some twenty meters straight down to the sand. He looked to the right—and there was the edge of a balcony that opened off the living room, as so many of the ocean-side apartments did. He could hear the loud music through the glass sliding doors, much better than through his sealed bedroom door.

The balcony was vacant, and heavy curtains concealed the interior of the living room. If he could reach it, and do so quietly . . . .

Harold moved back inside a little, braced one foot on the sill, and heaved out on the metal frame enclosing the glass. The catches broke with a loud shriek of tortured metal, and the whole pane swung upward. He sat on the sill, tilted his body far to the left while holding on with his right hand—and just missed grasping the bottom rail of the balcony.

Holding the edge of the window with both hands, Harold moved his buttocks out several centimeters—so far he would be immediately over-balanced if he let go. And then he released his grip and twisted his body hard to the left, before he had time to think, to hesitate . . . and both hands closed around the rail at the end of his swing.

Harold paused, breathing deeply of the warm air, feeling the sweat running wetly down his neck and chest. Then he transferred his grip to a vertical post and worked his way up hand over hand. Swinging his feet off the window sill, he clawed for a foothold on the bottom of the balcony. He found it and eased himself over the top rail, to collapse in a heap on the floor. Harold felt as if he had just conquered Mount Everest.

When the trembling in his muscles eased, Harold dragged himself to his feet. Jodie had been right; he *was* an office slug. The exercises he did at the health spa were not actually keeping him in good condition. At least the unusual feeling of fear and anxiety had vanished. Despite his physical fatigue, Harold felt his normal confidence in himself return. Now if he could just get off this balcony. . . . There was no way to reach the balcony above. With a sigh of resignation Harold crawled over the balustrade on the outer side, let himself down until he was hanging by his hands, and started swinging his legs. He was startled to find his grip slowly slipping, that his strength was inadequate to hold him there. On the next swing in he had to let go and plummeted down just inside the lower balcony railing. He landed in a heap and could not move.

There was a stir inside the lighted living room, someone coming toward the glass doors where the curtains were thrown wide to the night. A man peered out at Harold and hastily retreated. He came back with a pistol.

Harold raised both hands in abject surrender. 'Please! I'm not a burglar! I just escaped from upstairs. Some nuts up there, they were holding me—' he stopped, knowing he sounded incoherent.

'Wait. I'm not drunk or crazy. Will you call the police for me? You can hold me here until they arrive. Will you do that?'

The man, an elderly black with a few tufts of white hair and a deeply wrinkled face, looked puzzled. But he finally motioned for Harold to enter and lowered the pistol. 'Mister, I don't know who you are, or what's going on, but calling the police is one thing I *will* do! Now you just come inside and sit quietly 'till they come.'

Harold had never been so glad to obey a command in his life.

What he was surprised to discover, when the police finally arrived, was that they had no desire to go upstairs and summarily arrest the antitechs who had been holding him. They pointed out they had no search warrant and no proof beyond his word. When he finally convinced them and led the way upstairs, the officers' knock went unanswered. The room was now totally silent, and no light shone beneath the door.

When the manager was awakened and let the police in, Harold at least had the satisfaction of showing them the sound-proofed bedroom and bath, and the gaping hole through which he had escaped. And, finally, they accepted his word he was Harold Hentson, despite the fact he could offer no identification to prove it and was still wearing his wig. Since the kidnappers had already gone, they even agreed to let him fill out the reports on Monday and released him.

Harold caught an air taxi home in the pale light of early morning.

Lily had been called by the police. She was up and nervously pacing the floor when Harold walked in. 'Hal, what in the *world!* Pepi visied and tried to get me to call the police, but I felt—you know, that it might be embarrassing if they found you. I tried to tell him I was sure you were all right. And you were actually *kidnapped?* But there was no call for ransom or anything! I don't understand . . .'

'I'll explain it all later,' Harold said firmly. 'Did Pepi say how the launch preps were coming? Are we okay for this afternoon?'

'He mentioned going ahead just as if you were there. But he also said something I didn't understand, about Jarl being "fully in control". Hal—Are you sure our son is all right?'

'He's fine,' Harold assured her. 'Now I've got to get some sleep, or collapse. Pepi should be sleeping at the lab . . .' he visied the plant, and had the night switchboard operator put him through to the lab. Pepi was there. After he shook himself awake, Harold explained what had happened—leaving out his second identity—and asked for the present status.

'Everything's going very well, Hal. We took Jarl off medication and let the imprinted mind take full charge. He's sleeping naturally now. Jamison called a meeting this afternoon—yesterday afternoon, now—and agreed to push ahead just as if we were going to launch. But Fred Buck still says that injunction will be served, and we'll never get the bird off the ground.'

'I'll worry about that later. Listen, Pepi, relay some instructions for me. The group of antitechs who held me have something else planned, just in case RI went ahead with the launch. I want our security force beefed up. Call the guard captain and tell him I said put on double shifts all over Merritt Island. Put all three helicars in the air, and the two light planes. Place a heavy guard around Jarl. Close off the northern beaches if that hasn't been done, just in case some nut tries to get in there with a rifle. And clear the area of boats, both in the rivers and off-shore. Tell the shift captain to be ready for anything.'

'I'll get the security chief out of bed and let him do it,' said Pepi. 'And I'll call Jamison after breakfast and tell him you're back. When do you expect to get out here?'

'Let me sleep four hours . . . by noon at the latest. Call Jamison right now; he should be at the plant anyway. Tell him that bird lifts off on schedule or it's his head.'

'Gotcha!' Pepi said, with a broad smile on his round face. 'Go to sleep; always wanted to run Rockets International for a few hours anyway.'

'It's yours,' Harold assured him and punched off.

He did manage to brush his teeth before he collapsed, unbathed, into bed. He could not stand having his teeth feel coated.

* * *

Sunday, June 12, 2011

'How in living hell did he get away!' Jodie demanded angrily. 'Why didn't you hear him?'

Sergio looked uncomfortable. 'Well, we had the rooms sound-proofed, you know, so no one could hear our guests yelling. And Inez and Tanya brought over some records and a stereo, and we had a little party, you know—but Slippers stayed off the hi-lifters and so did I! It was just the noise that kept us from hearing him work on that bathroom window.'

'That was the third time we've used that place,' Strobe added. 'But Jesus was the first person we let walk in, and who knew where it was. We were going to have to move anyway.'

'That isn't the point!' snapped Jodie. 'We needed to keep him there until tonight! Now we'll have to go through with demonstrating on the island, which puts a lot of good people to work unnecessarily.'

'Nah, most of 'em will enjoy a Sunday march,' Strobe said cheerfully. 'I've just got to vise the squad leaders and tell 'em it's on.' She walked to her visiphone and started punching buttons.

'Sarcoma, I brought someone who has some interesting news,' Cindy Holcomb spoke up. They were sitting in Strobe's small livingroom, holding a hastily-called war conference. 'This is Bob Brown, the therapist for Jarl Hentson the Second. Tell her, Bob.'

'Well, I don't like to talk about the Hentson family—' the way he said it made it obvious Robert enjoyed nothing more—'but Hal has finally pulled a real raw one. He told Lily—Mrs. Hentson—that he wasn't going to do anything that could hurt young Jarl. But Inez and Cindy tell me he's supposed to be on that rocket, and it's a one-way trip. Now Lily doesn't have much backbone—but if she knew *that* she'd try to stop him!'

'Then go back and tell her! Maybe she'll join us at the fence. Jesus can burn her too when he launches the thing.'

'She'll just call the sheriff,' said Robert. 'Lily

almost never leaves the apartment.'

Jodie gave him a cold stare. 'Why don't you get on back and tell her anyway?'

Robert got up and hastily left.

'How many boats do we have on call, and of what capacity?' Jodie demanded of Sanderson.

'We have a hundred-and-five confirmed, and four probables,' the bearded engineer responded. 'Most of them are small, but we can crowd in eight or ten people for a short trip.'

'Good. The next item to check on is that injunction. Can you call that member who said he was a lawyer, ask him to contact any clerks he knows in the federal judge's office, see if the order has been written?'

Inez volunteered and left for her own apartment two floors up. Strobe was still busy calling FOE squad leaders around the Central Florida area. She was getting through to most, and the responses were uniformly good. Her contention that most members would enjoy a Sunday march was being confirmed.

In a quiet moment Jodie wondered how many members of FOE, and most of the other organized groups, participated out of a sense of boredom. It was certainly true she had gotten started that way, twelve years ago in college. Finishing the last two years had been difficult, and she hadn't even considered going for an advanced degree. Working in FOE, and two local college pressure groups, was far more interesting—and usually exciting. Most students struggled on because they had to face the necessity of supporting themselves. At least the Karlson millions had insulated her from that. And as long as Daddy didn't know about the Sarcoma identification, her allowance would stay adequate. She was an only child, and her mother had died while she was a baby. Her father professed an amused tolerance for the fact she chose to work in the low-paying field of Alternative Journalism. He would not have tolerated the illegal activities of her second alter-ego.

Inez returned in a few minutes with the news the injunction had been issued and was on its way to Merritt Island in the hands of a federal marshall. She also had some info not on the official paper—that it was not to be served until a half-hour before the launch. That would make it virtually impossible for RI to reach a higher judge and get the order cancelled in time—even if they could find one willing to act.

'Do you still think it's necessary to invade the island?' Inez asked. 'Even Jesus Hentson isn't going to risk a jail sentence for contempt.'

'We've already got the march in motion,' Jodie pointed out. 'And we'd better keep them coming, just in case Jesus is even crazier than we think.' She didn't add that calling it off now would not only spoil the fun of those who looked on this as a lark, but antagonize the serious ones who deeply believed in the antitech cause. It would also reflect badly on her judgement as a leader.

They were due to meet in the park at 1:00, and it was already past 11:00. Jodie went into the kitchen and made herself a sandwich. Strobe was still on the visiphone, and various FOE members were wandering in and out. Jodie went to her bedroom and dressed in a scarlet pantsuit, with a matching red wig, eyebrows, and eyelashes. She painted her lips a bright vermilion, rouged her cheeks heavily, and slipped on blood-red boots. It was time for Sarcoma to appear.

She felt the first gathering tingle of excitement, of joyful anticipation. Before she took off this wig again some male member of the local group was going to receive a pleasant surprise, a night to remember. He was going to make love with the legendary Sarcoma. That was the way she always ended an appearance, and there had been several over the past few years. Tomorrow it would be black-haired Jodie Carson who caught the Coastal Shuttle back to Boston.

But who would the lover be? None of the men she had closely associated with here appealed to her. Sergio and Bill were young and sloppy. Slippers had other inclinations.

Strange; she had met exactly one man who definitely moved her. She could understand why Diana Sharp had set herself up as a trophy for Jesus Hentson. Big Pig though he might be, at least he was a man of force and character. It was too bad he was on the opposite side—in fact the leader of it.

She could probably find someone in the crowd this afternoon.

9

Sunday, June 12, 2011

'We're ready to go, Jarl,' said Pepi.

Jarl patted his stomach—he had just finished a lunch three times the size he could remember eating as an older man—and rose from the table. He had awakened on this final morning with his mind almost clear, and for the first time had been allowed to walk to the simulator for the morning's practice run. Now it seemed very much as if he were simply young again, except that he had the experience of a full life to draw on. Fifty-six years of accumulated knowledge, and the body of a healthy young adult . . . he was no longer being bothered by that internal feeling of disturbed emotion, the odd and inappropriate upwellings that had difficulty expressing themselves in words. He seemed very much his old self.

No, strike that. A new young self. The gift of youth restored, except that it was temporary, would last two weeks . . . and somehow that did not seem fair. Such a short time to live . . .

Jarl followed Pepi out of the rear door of the lab and into a small aircar. It lifted off immediately for the launch site. There would be no dignitaries waiting to wave when he emerged from the suiting room, no huge crowd backed a safe five kilometers from the rocket. The Mars trip had been an unusual occurrence. Regular space flights had long been routine operations, which was the way Jarl preferred it. A Space Shuttle lifted off twice a week, to launch or service the various orbiting spacecraft, and a Big Bird with a huge section of the slowly growing Space Station roared skyward every month.

The Space Station had been his own idea, and he had rammed the initial planning money through Congress during his term. He had intended it to be a US venture. But after he left office the project had languished, Pepi had told him. It was only now coming to fruition, after Space Benefits had become a WorldGov agency.

Pepi had also told Jarl the political opposition had been intense, especially from the developing nations. They wanted all possible resources plowed into their own countries. The US and Russia—and strangely enough, China—had bulldozed the final authorization through the WorldGov Council.

Come to think of it, the Space Station authorization had been one of the main points raised against him in the 2004 election. The antitechs had exploited that one to the hilt, claiming it was useless and only an excuse to funnel government money to Rockets International. The fact he had given away every dime of RI stock had not influenced them. The 'gift' had been to his son—and most people would not accept it as genuine.

But it was. He had had no intention of returning to RI, much though he loved the company he had reorganized and built into a giant. The stock gift to Harold was irrevocable. And his son seldom asked his opinion after assuming the presidency. In fact they had gotten into minor conflicts a few times while Jarl was in office.

It was interesting to note the need for the Space Station had finally become obvious enough to convince even the sluggish WorldGov Council. NASA and RI had completed several pilot projects, demonstrating the economic feasibility of manufacturing everything from semipermeable membranes to vaccines in zero G. It must have been the dollars-and-cents figures on the reduced costs of producing perfect metal spheres for the hollow ball bearings that rolled in half the world's machines, or the casting of optically perfect lenses for telescopes and microscopes, that finally convinced them.

The same group of short-sighted nations had fought the establishment of an observatory on the back of the moon. But the astronomers and their university backers had been too powerful, worldwide. MoonEye had been built—and already had seen further into the depths of the universe than any ground-based reflector possibly could.

The aircar sat down on the roof of the old Vehicle Assembly Building. It was used primarily to assemble and check out the space Shuttles. Pepi and two watchful security guards led Jarl inside, down the open-face elevator to the 14th floor, and into the astronaut suiting room. Two RI technicians were on hand to help him into the spacesuit and check it out.

It felt good to be back in harness, to be grasping the portable oxygen bottle that would supply his air for the next two hours, to again be—an astronaut. Looking back from a unique perspective, Jarl almost chuckled aloud. How many people would think he was a nut to prefer the restricted life of a rocket jockey to the power and prestige accorded a United States President? Or even the president of Rockets International.

Jarl could say quite honestly he was more proud of being the first man to set foot on Mars than having held either position.

'Time to go, Jarl,' said Pepi, reappearing by his side.

It was 2:00. Now came the part he liked least, waiting on his back for two hours while the rocket and pilot's module underwent their final checks and tank-topping. But every job had its dull side.

The two security guards rejoined them when they emerged from the suiting room. Pepi led the way toward the elevator—and Lily Hentson came around the next corner and directly toward them, a man wearing a sheriff's badge following her.

'Jarl! What are you doing in that crazy suit! Stop this right now! Pepi Asturio, I don't know what you think you're doing, but you are *not* sending my son on any space flight! Sheriff—arrest him!'

The two security guards came to alert attention, looking curiously at Pepi. Lily hurried toward them, the unhappy-looking deputy sheriff in tow. 'Cut off the oxygen and undo my helmet,' Jarl said to the technician who had accompanied them.

'Not here, sir. Back in the suiting room, if that's what you want,'

'Put a facemask on her and the deputy and let them in,' ordered Jarl as he retreated inside, leaving Pepi to face the angry woman.

'Just a minute, Lily. I'm following Hal's directions, as I'm sure you know,' Pepi began. 'Where is he? If there's going to be any change in plans he has to okay it.'

'No he doesn't! This is my son as well as his! Mine more, because I've devoted my life to him. If you don't turn him over to me, and at once, I'll charge you with kidnapping! And I'll settle with Hal later. Right now I want my son!'

Pepi had never seen Lily Brewster Hentson so worked up before. She had always seemed a curious non-entity, a withdrawn and uncommunicative woman, devoted to her child and husband. In her own quiet way she had always been pleasant to him, and he got along well with her.

'Uhhh . . . I think you'd better do as she says, sir,' the deputy joined in. 'I understand that boy's retarded. If he isn't responsible for his own actions, and his father isn't here, then you're going to have to do what his mother asks.'

'No way, mister,' said Pepi simply.

The deputy's face flushed to dark red. His hand rather obviously moved toward his pistol. 'Now I'm telling you, mister, RI Big Pig or not—nobody's taking that retarded child out of here while his mother's standing there saying you can't do it! Now you just better turn him over to us, and right now, or there's going to be trouble.'

'Hal is supposed to be on his way here,' Pepi said to one of the security guards. 'Put in a call to dispatch and see if he can be located. Have them tell him it's an emergency. We're going to wait here.' He turned back to the deputy. 'We won't turn Jarl over to you, but we *will* wait until his father arrives. Lily, you may as well know. That isn't really your son now. It's your father-in-law, for all practical purposes. And you know damn well you aren't going to take the first Jarl Hentson anywhere he doesn't want to go.'

'That—that crazy imprinting thing? Nonsense, Pepi!' That's still my child. If you've messed up his mind that's something we'll settle later. Right now I just want him out of that spacesuit and back home.'

The suiting room door opened and a technician emerged. 'Mrs. Hentson, if you and the deputy will put on these face masks, you can come in and talk with . . . ah, Mr. Hentson.'

Lily gave him a puzzled look. No one 'talked' with her son. But she moved forward and took the mask, and the deputy followed.

Jarl had his helmet off. He refused to take the mask the technician offered; his face needed to be visible.

'Hello, Lily,' Jarl said aloud. 'You're looking well.'

There was a moment of stunned silence. Lily visibly faltered, one hand going to her hidden face. 'Jarl! How did you—did you . . .'

'Learn to talk? It would be very difficult to explain, Lily. Why don't you just accept that I'm really the first Jarl, not the son you knew. And I *am* going on board that rocket. I'm sorry, but too much depends on it—in ways you couldn't begin to understand.'

'Mrs. Hentson, he doesn't sound retarded to me!' the deputy broke in. He sounded puzzled. The fact Harold Hentson's son was a mental defective was common knowledge in the area.

'But it's still my son's body!' Lily cried. 'And this is a dangerous mission! You have no right to risk my son's body, I don't care what's in his mind!'

'Lily, I'm over eighteen years old,' Jarl said. 'Unless you have some court authority appointing you my legal guardian, I am a free adult. Do you have such—and if so, is it with you?'

Lily looked confused. 'Well of course there's paperwork! But Hal has it. He takes care of everything like that. Where is he? I thought he was coming here!'

The second security guard had returned, and been waiting for a chance to speak. 'Hal is on his way, Mrs. Hentson. Give him five minutes.'

Lily pulled the tattered shreds of her dignity around her and said, 'Then we will wait.' She seated herself in the only available chair. The deputy sheriff, looking extremely uncomfortable, remained standing, breathing heavily through the facemask.

It was ten minutes before Harold arrived. He had been conferring with Fred Buck on the best way to handle the expected injunction. Lily almost leaped to her feet, shouting. 'Hal, you lied to me!'

Harold crossed the room to the distraught woman, taking her hands in his. 'Yes, I did, Lily. I didn't want you to worry. I'm sorry someone told you—but this mission is too important to stop. Jarl is going.'

'Oh! Oh, I never could argue with you or your father!' And Lily collapsed into helpless tears, tearing the cloth off her face and flinging it to the floor.

* * *

Jodie glanced down the length of the rotting old Riverside Park dock. A motley swarm of jet-boats, cabin cruisers, launches—even some airboats and motorized sailboats—were tied up at every available point. Others waited off-shore. This park on the Indian River, just north of Titusville, was a state facility and popular with local residents. FOE would have to pressure Florida into better maintenance.

As each boat filled with passengers it pulled away from the dock, making room for those waiting. Jodie glanced at her watch. The loading would be completed by 3:00. Slippers, who owned one of the cabin cruisers, had assured her they could cross the river and walk to the launch pad in an hour. There was only one facility for the single-engine giant weight-lifter called the Big Bird, fronting the sea on the north tip of Merritt Island. They could get to within a few hundred meters by boat.

The antitech message center—which was three runners and a FOE member who had taken possession of the park's single public visiphone—had just sent word from Robert Brown that Lily Hentson had failed to reclaim Jarl. No one knew where the federal marshall was, nor when he planned to serve the injunction. It looked as if their bodies, the ultimate weapon that had served them so well in the past, would be the determining factor again. Now she felt vindicated in having organized the march.

'Sarcoma, the security guards across the river have noticed the unusual activity here and are keeping an eye on us,' a volunteer runner reported. 'And all the extra guards who were manning the roads to the south are being shifted north.'

'There won't be enough of 'em,' Jodie assured the young girl, who sounded frightened. 'Just remember; go limp, make them carry you away—and run back as soon as they release you. They couldn't possibly have enough handcuffs or vans to hold half of us.'

The girl nodded and sped away to get on one of

the last boats. Jodie checked the park for stragglers, waved to the girl at the visiphone and the young man with a fast boat who would wait with her, and walked to Slipper's cruiser. She was the last to board. Several people she did not know called greetings, and she nodded and smiled as she hurried up the ladder to the flying bridge. Slippers and Inez were in the two seats. The husky young woman hastily rose and offered her chair to Jodie.

'Run up the flag and let's move out,' Jodie ordered. Slippers nodded to someone standing by the short mast. As they backed away from the dock the bright red circle of the Friends of the Earth went
F
fluttering up, the FOE symbol prominent in black
E
in the center.

A ragged cheer burst from the surrounding boats. Jodie stood up—the top canopy was down and sun mercilessly bright and hot—and waved to the waiting people. Slippers eased them into open water, at idling speed, then gradually stepped up the pace. To avoid each others' wakes the following boats spread out in a vast half-circle. The awkward armada began moving across the six kilometers of open water to the northeast tip of the island.

Slippers had a pair of field glasses lying by the wheel. Jodie took them out of the case and turned toward Merritt Island. The towering bulk of the Assembly Building leaped into focus, far to the south. From this angle the attached Launch Control Center was hidden behind it, but she knew Jesus Hentson must be there, probably just getting the word they were about to be invaded. *And how are you going to stop this, Big Pig?* she asked silently over the distance that separated them.

* * *

Harold was too busy to listen for telepathic messages. He had a major problem on his hands.

'Mr. Hentson, your guards tried to stop me at the gate,' the paunchy, brown-faced man with the prominently displayed badge of a federal marshall said with controlled anger. 'They paid no attention to the writ-of-entry I have here from Judge Goodall. My associates placed them under arrest—after a little argument. Your front gate isn't being guarded now.'

'Yes it is, Mr. McDougal. The security chief sent two people to replace them,' Harold answered. They were standing in a glassed-in observation room of the Launch Control Center, where one of the four old firing rooms had been converted to handle the Big Bird vehicle. He did not add that the guards had tried to stop the marshall on his express orders, and with the assurance RI would be responsible for any legal difficulties their actions caused them.

'Well, I'm going to file charges against them for obstructing the legal work of a federal law officer.' McDougal reached into his jacket pocket—he wore an old-fashioned suit despite the heat of the day—and produced a folded paper. 'This is an injunction, signed by Judge Goodall, forbidding you to launch a rocket or make any other attempt to interfere with the interstellar probe thing that's due to go by the earth tonight. It is my duty to warn you that any violation of this order will result in the issuance of a bench warrant for your arrest. And I'm sure you know Judge Goodall doesn't look kindly on anyone brought before his court for contempt.'

Harold accepted the injunction and gave it to Fred Buck, who was standing by him. 'Okay, marshall, you've done your duty. I've accepted the injunction, and it's in effect. Now why don't you get back to Orlando and enjoy your Sunday afternoon.'

The marshall looked surprised. 'Go back? No sir, I'll be waiting right here. If that rocket goes off, the judge will want to know how many of you he has to put in jail. That order applies to Rockets International as a whole, not just you.'

Harold shrugged. 'In that case, have a seat and watch. Just don't try to interfere with our work—or you'll need the whole US Internal Peace Force to keep you from being thrown out of here!'

McDougal stiffened. 'If I need the Peace Force, Mr. Hentson, I can get it! And I will.'

'Sit down,' said Harold wearily and walked away.

'Hal, I hope you appreciate just how serious this is,' Fred Buck said low-voiced as he followed. 'You, the technicians here, young Jarl—you can all be jailed for years if that judge finds you in contempt!'

Even a contempt citation can be appealed. We'll take him to a higher court.'

'Yes, it can be appealed, but I'll tell you now it would do no good. Judges are notorious at sticking together on matters pertaining to their authority. And the Supreme Court would never agree to review the case. My professional advice—and my urging as a friend, Hal—is to stop the launch.'

'I hear you, Fred; thanks.' Harold walked down

into the firing room proper, and stopped by the security console. 'What's the latest on that fleet of boats heading this way?'

'The aircars report it's a large group of pleasure boats, Hal,' the shift security chief responded. 'The leader is flying a round red flag, the symbol of the Friends of the Earth. They seem to be headed northeast at about eight knots, which will get them to the pad in just a few minutes.'

'Is there any way to stop them?'

The security woman shrugged. 'Our pilots are armed with pistols and rifles. There's no way we could sink a boat or even disable one without probably killing people. And I don't think you want that.'

'No I don't. What about after they land? Do we have enough guards to keep them a safe distance away from the pad?'

'I've called in every person I can possibly spare from the south end. We have over a hundred guards gathering on the shore, and about thirty assorted vehicles. The only way to stop them is to arrest them for trespassing and haul 'em away. I doubt if we can get the area cleared before the launch. In fact I *know* we can't.

'Rush some more vehicles up there. Call out the firemen. Tell them to bring every truck, including the hovertanks. When the demonstrators wade to shore, take them into custody, carry them at least ten klicks from the pad, and send the vehicle back for more. Skip the usual arrest procedures.'

'Okay, Hal; but it won't be enough.'

'Tell the guards to work as fast as possible. I'm told there won't be any resistance if the FOE people follow their usual tactics. Just haul them away and get back for another load.

Harold glanced at the huge wall clock; it was nearing 4:00. Barely half an hour to go. The security chief was right. Jodie/Sarcoma and her friends had planned well.

A sudden thought occurred to Harold. There was a possibility the invading army had overlooked. He hurried to the console of the launch conductor and demanded, 'Wilson! Could you launch that bird now? Right, now, within the next three minutes?'

The engineer looked startled. 'No; no, Hal. The tanks are still being topped and the radio interference checks aren't complete. Fifteen minutes, maybe. If you had given me an hour's notice of a change. . . .'

'The good ideas come too late,' Harold said, turning away. 'Carry on then,' Fifteen minutes would see most of the FOE crowd standing next to the fence, patiently waiting to die if Jesus Hentson decided to launch his futile suicide mission rocket. A matter that was looking increasingly doubtful.

Harold walked to the spacecraft communications console. He saw the alert face of his son staring out at him from the small TV screen—a face physically similar to the one he had known for years and yet subtly different.

'Let me take your place a few minutes,' Harold said to the technician.

The man looked surprised but obediently removed his headset and rose. Harold slipped it on and sat down.

'Hello again, Jarl,' he said aloud. There had been no time to talk in the suiting room.

Harold saw his father/son look toward his own

console. The wall-mounted camera threw his face into an upper left profile on Harold's screen. Jarl gave him a wicked grin. 'What say, Wild-Hair. Looks as if you've really got one up it this time.'

Harold hadn't heard that scatalogical nickname in years. Only his father had ever used it in public.

'Yeah, this project has brought on a few problems. Just wanted to tell you a small army of antitechs is landing on the shore just beyond the pad. It's doubtful we can clear them away in time to launch.'

'Yes, I've been watching them since the first boats came into my view. Quite a little navy they have there. What are you going to do about it?'

'We'll transport them south of the Assembly Building as fast as possible. But it doesn't look good. We *could* have launched earlier and made the rendezvous a little sooner, at the cost of a little extra propellant. But I didn't think of it in time.'

'They plan to stand around the fence, I presume? Harold, misguided fools or not, you can't kill all those people. I hate to see a Hentson whipped, but I think you've had it.'

'That's the general consensus of opinion.' Harold was silent a moment, then added, 'Look on the good side. If you don't make it, we will have a little time together.'

'And save the life in this healthy young body.' Jarl nodded. 'But I don't . . . really want to stick around for just a few days. Not unless I can do something useful. Did you know I had my predecessor's persona brought back when I was President? It was the usual computer simulation, and I tried to ask the so-called "personality" some questions. He gave me answers all right, but they were useless. Somehow the simulation didn't seem . . . quite as whole a person as I am.'

'It probably wasn't. You're the first to be imprinted on a human brain where the circuits were both blank and genetically similar to you. We seem to have proved this part of my idea works—but its general application is going to be pretty limited.'

'I certainly hope so!' Jarl replied. he glanced at a side screen and said, 'Well, I see the guards are hauling them off. But you've only got thirty minutes. You'll never make it, Wild-Hair.'

10

Sunday, June 12, 2011

Jodie drifted through the crowd, watching the uniformed guards collaring and hauling away the demonstrators. Some of the men went limp and had to be carried. Most of the women disdained to be touched, even by the female guards, and walked to the various vehicles. Those who were placed in vans with locking doors could not get out—but there were several other types of vehicles there, from hovertank fire trucks to small steamies. And where the guards had no way of confining them, the people were sneaking back the instant the arresting officer turned his back.

'We've got 'em whipped, Sarcoma!' Strobe called jubilantly. She was pressed to the fence next to Slippers. Jodie was walking around the pad, trying to escape the attention of the security guards. They were concentrating first on the people actually holding to the wire, leaving her alone at the moment.

Jodie waved to Strobe and kept walking. She knew her costume made her a conspicuous figure, but these guards had no way of knowing she was the leader of the group. Most of them would automatically assume some man was in charge, even the women in security. Male chauvinism was far from dead in the world.

The first full van started up and roared away, carrying about twenty people jammed inside. The huge hovertanks could carry a hundred if necessary, but the guards had no way of confining them. For the moment they were concentrating on filling the vans. It was obviously futile, but corporation security personnel were paid to act, not think. And they had their orders.

* * *

Harold Hentson was paid to think. As he was sitting and talking to Jarl, word came that the first van of demonstrators had been hauled away. He glanced at the clock. It was 4:15. Not a single truck would have time to return for a second load.

But fifteen minutes was time enough to clear the area, if everyone left willingly. They could get far enough away to be safe, even if at some damage to their eardrums.

And suddenly Harold had a wild idea. If those demonstrators could be panicked into running . . .

He hurried to the launch conductor's console. 'Wilson! Can we fire the vernier rockets on the Big Bird separately? Say for about three or four minutes?'

'Sure, Hal, by taking it off automatic sequence and using the override system. But what's the point of that?'

'Never mind. Just stand ready to do so on my signal. I want to start one, then the other. Give me a mike and patch me into the pad loudspeaker system.'

Wilson passed his desk microphone to Hal and flipped two switches on his console. He turned a dial and said, 'That's maximum volume. I'll set up for the override.'

Harold seized the microphone.

* * *

"LISTEN YOU STINKING FREAKS!" an amplified voice rolled out over the pad area, coming from speakers set in the fence and throughout every building. *'Listen, damn you, if you want to live! This is Jesus-Son-of-God-Hentson! I'm going to fire that rocket! You hear me? If you stay there you're going to burn, goddamn you! I'm going to watch your lousy asses fry!'*

The voice was screaming high, wild, filled with rage and hate. It rasped on the ears like a file. Jodie felt the anger and hatred as an almost palpable presence, thickening the air around her. It did not sound like Hal Hentson at all.

'You've got one minute, you scum! Just one minute, and I'm going to burn you! Start running if you want to live! Get on those trucks! Wade to the boats if you can but get going! This is no bluff! I repeat, this is no bluff!'

Jodie whirled toward the distant blocky tower of the Assembly Building. 'Don't listen!' she shouted, her voice lost in the sudden hubbub. 'Don't believe him, he *is* bluffing! Stay where you are! But only a few people standing near at hand could hear her.

'LAST CHANCE!' the voice thundered. 'NOW YOU CAN BURN!'—and suddenly there was a deeper rumble. Flame belched from the base of the rocket, on the side toward Jodie. It was half a kilometer from the fence to the rocket but the rising crescendo of sound smote at her ears with painful intensity.

Screams of fright filled the air. Even the guards

looked terrified. There was a panicked rush for the vehicles. Several of the drivers started their engines, ready to race away, but the voice of Harold Hentson came rolling out again. 'DRIVERS! Wait for loads! Let those on who want to live! Cover your ears and wait!'

Those people nearest the shore were dashing through the shallow water to the boats, anchored several meters out. The rocket that was firing on the Big Bird continued to hurl sound and fire into the flame trench; the air around the pad grew hazy with smoke.

Almost a thousand struggling, screaming people tried to scramble on or in the huge firetrucks and other vehicles. The guards and firemen were a disciplined crew; they waited. Jodie ran with the second wave, urging anyone she could grab to stop. 'Don't go! He's lying, it's just the little rockets! Stay here! He won't dare! . . .' but no one was listening.

Two boats started and almost immediately went to cruising speed. Several people were left floundering in the water. Four more pulled out, but one angled back in to pick up the people who were left. A huge hovertank, with people clinging and holding to every available protuberance, rose on its air curtain and moved toward the road, gathering speed.

Fire burst from the other side of the rocket, and the noise level doubled. Jodie put her hands over her ears and discovered her body was shaking slightly from the vibration—but the sound was bearable. Someone came running by her, a familiar face: Strobe. The tall woman was fleeing in wild-eyed panic. She screamed, her voice near hysteria. And after a few more steps she reached an open-bodied truck and climbed on to the exposed rubber tire. Hands grasped her wrists and yanked her up to the flat floor.

Jodie saw that several older people had fallen in the rush. Some younger ones stopped and dashed back to help them. A van roared away toward the road—whether full or with a scared guard at the wheel she could not tell. Engines were revving up all around her. More and more people piled on, and the vehicles fleeing the area became a steady stream.

Jodie glanced toward the water. Every person who had elected to escape by boat was on board one and leaving. Half the vehicles on land were gone, with several of the others starting to move. And most of the demonstrators were riding away, the rest fighting to get aboard the last few cars and vans.

The rockets had been firing steadily for four minutes now, and the Big Bird hadn't lifted off. But the steady beat of the sound still tore at her ears when she removed her hands in disgust. It didn't seem to have dawned on the crowd it was long past time the engines reached full thrust and the vehicle rose from the pad.

A mob did not think. Once set in motion, it proceeded with blind relentlessness toward whatever it had elected to do. Jodie had used this characteristic often in the past. Now Jesus Hentson had turned it against her.

Jodie discovered she was the only person not already on board a truck or trying to reach one. It was amazing how fast a thousand people could move when it was over open ground and to a widely dispersed group of vehicles.

She turned and looked at the fat bulk of the

rocket, towering almost two hundred meters into the air. Through the smoke and flame from the verniers she saw that the huge bell of the single main engine was cold and inert. She stood and stared at it, wanting it to ignite, to brighten and roar into the terrible sound that could shatter eardrums, rattle bones in their sockets, ultimately kill—if the flames and heat didn't reach this far first.

And then two women in guard's uniforms were grasping her arms, pulling her away. She saw that both wore ear protection. These women had guessed what the FOE people had not, that the small rockets might thunder and pound at them for an hour, but the main engine was not going to ignite until they were safely down the road.

Jodie gave up and went with them peacefully. No, Jesus Hentson was not bluffing. He was going to launch the bird as he had said—because he had succeeded in scaring these people into retreating. There would have been no launch if he had failed.

The two women hustled Jodie into a cab with themselves, and the firetruck whirled away and down the road in a snarling of gears.

* * *

The security chief was playing her highest camera over the pad area. 'It's working, Hal!' she called, trying to restrain her excitement. 'And I talked with our dispatcher. He got word to all the drivers with radios not to leave until they had full loads. By God! we're going to make it!'

'Not quite,' said Harold, glancing at the clock. It was 4:34, and the automatic sequencer took three minutes to fire after activation. 'But close enough to be within the window.'

Harold walked swiftly to the observation room,

where McDougal sat dourly watching the busy men at their consoles. The marshall could see the small verniers firing on the giant screens provided on the wall, and that the bird hadn't left the pad.

* * *

'I'll be damned!' Jarl said aloud when he felt the engine ignite almost two hundred meters below. 'I believe that crazy son of mine has pulled it off!'

It was good to ride a rocket once more, to feel the familiar shuddering vibration shaking the chair in which he was strapped—and a few seconds later the jar when the holddown clamps released, and the instant surge upward as the vehicle rose off the pad.

There was a metal plate over the pilot's window, but the launch technicians were feeding a picture of the liftoff to his console. Jarl warched in wonder as the tail cleared the tower, the huge engine nozzle belching the widest flame he had ever seen. This monster made the Space Shuttle he was accustomed to riding seem small. He checked his instruments. That was all he had to do at the moment, monitor and report anything that seemed out of the ordinary. That at least hadn't changed since he last flew. But it was only a short time before Harold's face appeared on the screen, and the flaming tail he was seeing disappeared.

'Hey, old man, how do you like that for a liftoff?'

'Not bad for a one-burner. Did you get all those people far enough away or lose a few eardrums?'

'Don't know yet. I'm sure no one was seriously hurt, though. How did you like my acting? I sounded so mean and believable I even scared the launch crew! But listen, I just called to remind you

I had the easy part and it's done. The rest is up to you.'

'Thanks lots,' Jarl said—and realized Harold was saying nothing but the obvious truth. The toughest part of this mission, with all its unknown dangers, still lay ahead—and he alone would bear the responsibility for its success or failure.

'Will you come with me, please?' Harold asked, grasping the man's arm.

'What for? What do you want?'

'I want you to serve as a witness for an illegal act. Hurry, please; this is important.'

The marshall reluctantly followed Harold to the launch director's console. 'Wilson, show this man the automatic sequencer switch.'

Looking puzzled, Wilson touched a tiny switch on his console face, similar to many others except that its plastic covering was a shiny red in color.

'Is everything else ready?' demanded Harold.

'It has been for ten minutes. The engine would have ignited on time if I hadn't taken it off automatic, as you ordered.'

'Good. Marshall McDougal, please notice. I, and I alone, am going to throw the switch that will cause engine ignition and liftoff in three minutes. I take full responsibility for my action. Neither Wilson nor anyone else shares the blame with me.'

And with that Harold flipped the little red switch.

'You're going to suffer for that, Mr. Hentson,' said the officer, his voice grim. 'I don't suppose I can stop anyone who deliberately defies a federal judge's order—but you'll have a long time in jail to be sorry you did that.'

'Probably,' Harold agreed. The thought of prison deeply disturbed him, but if that was the price for this launch, he had no choice but to pay it. 'For now, let's watch liftoff on the big screen.'

'You're a cool customer, Mr. Hentson,' said McDougal. 'Now I guess I know why they call you Jesus—you think you can get away with anything.' They sat down in the comfortably padded chairs and watched the tall rocket, the two streams of fire from the verniers still pouring down into the flame trench.

And two minutes later, well within the twenty minute launch window, a small cloud of blue-white fire gushed from the center of the huge bell-shaped main engine. The fire grew, spread, brightened intolerably, until the camera could no longer convey the message of its whiteness—and great holding arms retracted, and another Big Bird rose majestically off the pad on a pillow of flame.

* * *

Jodie's truck was four kilometers down the road when the earth began shaking under them, and a brightness like a second sun rising bloomed on the ground to their rear. Jodie twisted her head to peer past the driver's shoulder. She had to squint her eyes to protect them from the rising glare as the largest rocket engine on earth slowly lifted the Big Bird off the pad and into the tortured air. The gleaming white capsule on top, with an odd skeletal framework she had never seen on Tri–D extending ahead of it, rose above the smoke and vapor. And then the giant rocket picked up speed, its finned base and the massive stream of fire below it climbing above the umbilical tower. And seconds later it was past the angle Jodie could see through the window and out of sight—but the sound of its passage still rocked and shook them, like a giant hand playing with toys.

PART III

From the Master's Thesis scrapbook of Jarl Hentson

But if we allow these Planetary Inhabitants some sort of Reason, must it needs, may some say, be the same with ours? Certainly it must; whether we consider it as applied to Justice and Morality, or exercised in the Principles and Foundations of Science. For Reason with us is that which gives us a true Sense of Justice and Honesty, Praise, Kindness, and Gratitude: 'tis That that teaches us to distinguish universally between Good and Bad, and renders us capable of Knowledge and Experience in it. And can there be any where any other Sort of Reason than this? or can what we call just and generous, in Jupiter and Mars be thought unjust Villany?

Christianus Huygens: New Conjectures Concerning the Planetary Worlds, Their Inhabitants and Productions (c. 1670)

11

Sunday, June 12, 2011

'Mr. Hentson, the Judge will be in his chambers tomorrow at 9:00, and about 9:01 I'll be heading back this way with a warrant. Where can I expect to find you?'

Harold smiled at McDougal. 'The plants are closed on Monday, but I'll be in my office by 10:00, to watch the contact. I'll wait for you there.'

'Mr. Hentson, you won't be the first Big Pig I ever arrested,' the federal officer went on conversationally. The two men were walking out of the Launch Control Center toward the parking lot. 'Once back in the nineties I took in old man Roger Woodall, while he was head of GM. They refused to obey a federal judge's order to shut down a factory that was polluting the air, and we didn't waste any time with the Little Pigs—went right to the top.'

'Yes, I read about it. And I also remember the order was appealed all the way to the Supreme Court and finally overturned there. The district judge had exceeded his authority in ordering that plant closed without the required hearings.'

'Yessir. But they upheld a separate charge of contempt against Mr. Woodall, for refusal to obey a lawfully issued court order.'

'For which he paid some small fine,' Harold agreed. They were at the marshall's steamie.

'And you think that's just what you're going to do, don't you?'

'I hope so, but I don't really know. It doesn't matter. I did what I had to do. After that, you take your chances.'

'Mr. Hentson, you aren't going to like it in jail,' said McDougal. He started his vehicle, waited sixty seconds, and drove away.

As Harold looked to the west he saw one of the last firetrucks pulling into the southwest parking lot, its long body covered by a clinging swarm of people. A guard stepped down out of the cab, followed by a short figure in a bright scarlet pantsuit. There was something familiar in the smooth, easy way she moved. Harold made a hasty search, found a company steamie with the key inside, and appropriated it. Three minutes later he was pulling into a parking space near the milling crowd.

One of the guards spotted him and came hurrying over. 'Mr. Hentson?—uh, Hal! Now that we've got 'em here, what are we supposed to do?'

'Give the firemen back their vehicles. Use the vans and steamies to get all those back to their boats who want to go. See to it they leave the land. Tell those who want rides into Merritt Island to wait, and start running them down to Orlando Expressway when you have a free vehicle.'

The guard hurried away to relay the orders. The apparent mass confusion slowly began to untangle as people decided where they wished to go. Most chose to return to the boats, but several knew they had lost their ride. They accepted transport back to the major east-west highway.

This crowd had cleared away from the launch pad in ten minutes, but it took them an hour to leave the parking lot. Harold kept watching for the bright form of their leader, but Jodie/Sarcoma had disappeared. Probably afraid he would have her arrested on sight.

Harold did see Strobe and the young man named Sergio. The tall woman noticed his glance and resolutely looked the other way. Sergio looked frightened. Harold let them leave without a word.

When only the area patrol guard remained, Harold started the company steamie and headed for the exit on to the state highway. As he was passing through the gate a throaty voice behind him said, 'Congratulations, Jesus.'

Harold jerked forward, so startled he almost lost control of the car. Jodie laughed. 'What's the matter? Nerves a little tight? Stop worrying; we aren't going to put you back in a cell. The Feds will do that for us tomorrow.'

Harold risked a glance over his shoulder. She was sitting up in the rear, obviously after hiding on the floorboard. There was no weapon in sight. And as he stared, Jodie deftly eased over the front seatback and slid down beside him.

'Cocoa Beach, please. And hurry; I have to get to a bathroom.'

Harold eased out into the sparse Sunday afternoon traffic. 'What makes you think I won't turn you over to the police?'

'I saw you recognize Strobe and Sergio and let them go.'

Harold was silent. The antitechs had already proven they knew his personal habits. Jodie was proving she understood his temperament as well.

'Incidentally, you've only won the first battle,' Jodie went on. 'My people tell me your own brains at RI have assured you the odds against Jarl Hentson being able to stop the Probe are awfully high. And even if he does, WorldGov or ourselves will have you put away by the time it returns. You aren't going to get that second rocket you need off the ground.'

'I'll worry about that when I know we need it.'

'You *are* a stubborn one. But that just makes fighting you more fun.'

Harold turned left at the intersection to Cocoa Beach. They were silent for the few minutes it took to cross Merritt Island and turn south. He was trying to understand this strange but still very attractive woman sitting by him. She enjoyed what she was doing, whereas most protestors he had met seemed grim and determined fanatics, True Believers in the worst sense of the word. There was an unusual vitality, an impressive life-force in this woman, one which should have been directed toward more worthwhile ends.

'Where can I drop you?' Harold asked as they entered the edge of Cocoa Beach, which straggled along the highway from the southeast gate of the Kennedy Space Center to the edge of the Patrick Internal Peace Base.

'Your secret apartment is in the Royal Twins, isn't it? And steam along, I'm about to wet these scarlet pants.'

Harold steamed along.

It was almost dark when they reached his apartment. Jodie stayed inside the bathroom over half an hour, and Harold heard the shower running in the relaxorbath.

It was no surprise when the door finally opened and Jodie stood there nude. There was something very primitive and direct in her eyes.

'Still want to settle this thing between us man-to-woman?' she asked, almost casually.

Harold felt his throat go dry. He was not stupid enough to think he could compete in sexual athletics with a woman ten years his junior, nor with a woman of any age who wanted to use her body as a weapon. But that scarcely mattered. Here, as always, it was the joy found in struggle that counted.

Harold openly stared at Jodie. Some of his bought mistresses had been younger and more beautiful—but this was the most desirable woman he had ever known.

Harold was suddenly conscious of the fact he hadn't had a bath since Friday, that he had a two-day growth of beard, and was terribly hungry. He began shedding clothes—but walked toward the bathroom as he did. It was her turn to wait while he had a shower and shaved.

* * *

Monday, June 13, 2011

Jarl awoke from a hard sleep to find his neck stiff and his strong body growing increasingly weary of the constant weight of three G's. One zero G period had been built into the flight plan, but it had been shortened by lifting off late in the launch window.

He glanced at the chronometer and saw it was 6:00 Eastern Daylight time. He had slept for five hours. And that was his second sleep period of the night. Rendezvous was to be about 11:00 this morning.

Jarl had to call Mission Control to alert them that he was awake. There was no electroencephalograph built into this operational helmet.

'Ready for some breakfast, Jarl?' the controller asked when he came on. It was the same smooth young snot who had first led him through his paces in the simulator.

'Hell yes; I'm starved, as always.'

'You'll have to prepare your own this time. The wall unit to your right is both a refrigerator and oven. Open the bottom door . . .' and the efficient young man led him step by step through the preparation of the usual frozen dish. This vehicle was intended only for short Earth-orbit flights and not designed for pilot comfort.

When Jarl finished, the young controller said, 'Let's run through the attitude positioning exercises once more, Jarl, using the real controls. The results will be simulated, of course; we've got you cut off here. We'll feed the data into the flight computer and give you the projected results on your main screen.'

Jarl went to work. He could feel old skills growing sharper with each practice session. Strange, how much came rushing back when the right associations were exercised. And the odd, unexplainable upwellings of feeling that seemed foreign to his nature had ceased to bother him. He felt very much as though he was a complete being. But of course those parts of his memory that were missing simply did not exist, and he would have no way of knowing they were absent.

They were already far enough from earth that a

time lapse of several minutes was required for sending and receiving signals, forcing Jarl to pause after each action to await the result. But they were uniformly good good when they came. The sensitivity required in handling a spaceship in zero G had returned.

There was a long break after Jarl finished the exercises, with Mission Control available but not talking. Jarl had little to do, and his thoughts turned to the oddity that was himself. It seemed strange that he would exist only for two weeks, when he felt almost normal. It was stranger yet that he should be here, on a suicide mission. He had always been a life-oriented person. But the logic of the peculiar circumstances had forced him into a decision he would not normally have made.

If he could live for only two weeks, and there was a chance he could do a truly great deed for humanity in that time, he had no choice but to try. The only sad part was that his grandson's body had to die, and there was nothing he could do about it.

* * *

Harold was also thinking.

They had gotten up at 6:00 and gone out for breakfast, then returned and promptly headed for the bed. They fell asleep after making love, but Harold soon awoke and lay looking at the slumbering face of Jodie. She slept with her mouth slightly open, breathing slowly but deeply. There were wrinkle marks at the corners of her eyes, and small lines on the neck. She was not a young woman. But the fire and intensity he had sensed in her had come out full-force in love-making. He had lost every contest during the night, as expected—but they had occurred as part of the most joyous struggle he had ever waged. Harold realized he had never met anyone at all like her—and his life had been the poorer for it.

Jodie opened her eyes.

The veil of sleep cleared away. She blinked several times and sat up, stretching and yawning. She glanced at her watch. 'You aren't going to be in your office to meet the marshal at 10:00 unless you get moving.'

'The actual contact will be sometime after 10:30. I think I'll send him word to wait and watch it from Launch Control. He might try to carry me away before we know the results. Would you like to come along?'

'Good gosh, no! I can't afford to be seen with you in public! And I'm expecting you to live up to your so-called "gentleman's code" and never mention this night to anyone. We both had the urge, we satisfied it—and now we can go back to our separate lives.'

Harold had learned, during the night, just how separate those lives were. During some of the long hours of quiet talking, between the arousing and satisfying of passion, Jodie had revealed a great deal about herself and her ideas. They were completely alien to Harold's experience, jarring in their totality of opposition to what he believed.

'We exist as artificial entities, self-created human artifacts,' Jodie had said, sitting up in bed and drinking from a glass on the bookend headboard. 'The machines have separated us from our senses, so that we perceive with only half our ability. We are only half alive.' The curtains were drawn back from the single window, letting small fingers of moonlight into the shadowed room. In front of the building the Atlantic tumbled in phosphorescent splendor toward the beach—but they could not see the water from the bed.

'We are so proud of civilization, of our great machines and our mighty industries. But in fact, the most primitive savage left in the Amazon jungle is more alive than a corporation president—such as yourself. That savage *feels* with his hands. He *smells* the world around him—both the pleasant and the foul. He is *aware* that he exists, and in harmony with his environment. Every moment of the day, he *lives!* Can you understand me? His life is richer, more full than yours and mine because he exists at a higher level of intensity. He *uses* his body constantly, and with him, muscle and mind are one.'

'Then you reject the oldest teachings on which western civilization is based, the dichotomy between mind and body formulated by the Greek philosophers? You equate sharper physical senses and stronger muscles with quality of life? Then the elephant must be superior to Man—he's certainly stronger and has better senses—and the lion must live more intensely.'

'But of course! *All* the wild animals lead lives more satisfying than ours! They live as nature intended and have no troubles caused by intellect. Yet they have all the intelligence needed to survive within their world.'

Harold could only shake his head in wonder. There was no doubting her sincerity. 'Then what you would really like is to see civilization fall, forcing us to return to living in the woods. Our lives might be shorter when the tigers came hunting, but we'd live more "intensely".'

'Exactly! But I don't tell even my most devoted FOE friends what I've just told you. Even they don't carry logic to its end, see the final result we should be striving for. I concentrate on the space program because it's easy to show how wasteful and corrupt it is, and how little it returns for all the money and effort. But they think in terms of devoting those resources to more worthwhile projects. I don't. The technology the space program has spawned should die, not be transmogrified.'

'You use a lot of words that stand for very abstract concepts. Would they exist in this primitive world you're describing? Could you even make this argument without the words?'

'If we were total primitives there would be no need for the abstract. The concepts would not exist, nor would they be missed.'

'I doubt that.' Harold was quiet for a moment, then said, 'Let me tell you a story my father told me when I was a small boy. Yes, he held me on his lap and told me stories, just like any other father and son, if that's what brought that skeptical expression to your face. The publicity gimmick you people came up with of calling that man "God" Hentson—' Harold shook his head at the absurdity of it. 'Anyway, it happened during his second year of college.

'An Indian Yogi visited Harvard and lectured to the class. He was the genuine article, not one of your thousand American imitators. He let the physiologists strap him into various machines and demonstrated how he could control his breathing, slow or speed up his heartbeat at will, expand or contract the large intestine, and so on. He had attained what you described as awareness of the body. The instructor called it partial command of the autonomous nerve system. And of course the Yogi told them how important self-understanding was, and presented himself as a man who had devoted years of his life to practicing internal physiological control. He said he could do things with his body Westerners couldn't, and proved it. He made it all seem very impressive. He was also a man at peace with himself. Father said he had a sort of gentle air about him, a calm self-possession the students envied. He must have been about fifty at the time, and appeared to have no worries or cares. He refused to accept money except for his expenses. And everyone thought that surely this was a man to be emulated.'

Harold stopped, lost in thought. 'Go on,' Jodie prompted.

'During his second week there he was demonstrating internal cleanliness—where he sucked water up into the large intestine, swirled it around, forced it back out—when he got a very surprised look on his face and stopped. He appeared to be in pain. He got out of the tub and dried himself off. Dad noticed he was leaning forward slightly, unable to stand upright. The rest of the class left, but the next period was a free one for father, and he hung around. The ambulance came for the Yogi a few minutes later. He was taken to the university hospital and operated on for a burst appendix.'

Harold took a long swallow of his drink. 'Oh, the story has a happy ending. The operation was successful, though the Yogi had waited too long while attempting to "cure" himself by internal control—which did include the ability to ignore pain. He recovered his health, finished his tour, and went back to India. But the incident made my father think. All those years devoted to patiently developing control over the nerves of his large intestine—and when trouble came, in a vestigial remnant of it called the vermiform appendix—he couldn't do a thing for himself. An appendectomy is a very simple operation by our medical standards —but he would have died without it.'

'So-o-o? He probably lived five real lives within his fifty years, compared to Jarl Hentson—or that surgeon who saved him, or you for that matter.'

'I can't believe that. But the point of the story is that science and technology are life-enhancing, not life-destructive. By gaining control over the external, material world, we achieve a far greater ability to correct malfunctions within our own bodies. Plus the benefits of a steady food supply and freedom from enemies, the other primary needs internal control can't provide.'

Jodie was a small dark body leaning back against the headboard. He could just make out the soft blur of white skin, see the darker tangle of black hair behind her head. She leaned forward to kiss him lightly, a prelude to the regeneration of passion, and said, 'The Yogi is probably dead now, along with the surgeon, and neither of them could have convinced the other, and nor will you or I. When your marvelous science can show me a *long* life—say about ten-thousand years—then I'll accept that as a substitute for a more fulfilling and intense one.'

'If we are to have a chance at immortality it will come through science, not Yogi,' said Harold—but the soft lips returned to cover his, and for a time he again lived very intensely, and without words.

12

Monday, June 13, 2011

'Jarl?' The smooth-faced young controller was back. 'We have a good radar track on you both and are allowing for the time lag. Once you've turned around and aligned yourself in its path, you will start by going into full reverse thrust. As the Probe comes to you, ease off. If it takes evasive action, move to the opposite side and let it pass. We'll start up the main drive again and try to get close enough to disable the engines with your laser.'

'Wouldn't it be safer and simpler to come up behind it and hit those engines in the first place?'

'We'd rather have them undamaged, if possible. It's about three klicks to your right at the moment. Move your right window shield and take a look.'

When the metal plate slid aside Jarl saw the Probe. Sunlight outlined an ovoid shaped like a gigantic egg, large and leading. The angle of travel let the light reach past the center of the rounded nose, so that the side toward him was partially lighted in front but otherwise in deep shadow. The color was a bright and shining silver.

The two engines at the tapered rear were partially inset within the line of the body, only the nozzles breaking the symmetry. They seemed small for such a bulky ship but produced a giant cloud of blue fire. Jarl wondered what design considerations had led the alien builders to select such low-thrust devices. Were there advantages Earth engineers had overlooked because of the limited burn-time available on all prior rocket engines?

'Your main drive will be stopping in about two minutes, Jarl. Start the right yaw maneuver as soon as you lose power. While we're waiting, go ahead and set your maneuvering engines for reverse thrust.'

Jarl complied and settled down to the remembered task of piloting a spaceship. He was on his own now. The time-lag was too great for help from Mission Control.

The timing was virtually perfect. When he completed the turn and found himself looking through the spidery skeleton of the attach fitting, Jarl was less than two kilometers from the Probe. From this front position the visitor did not seem large or impressive enough to be an interstellar vehicle. But it was far more advanced than anything Earth could produce when he had been an astronaut. Or even when he had . . . Jarl chopped off that thought. Death was not a part of his memory. There was no need to dwell on the fact it had happened.

The gap between the two ships was swiftly narrowing. Jarl started the two maneuvering engines and eased them up to full thrust. The drag he had momentarily lost returned, though at less than one G. After a moment the distance between the two ships seemed to stabilize. He cut power slightly, waited—then cut it again. The Probe came steadily forward, the cloud of dark blue fire filling space behind it.

Jarl let it gain on him, trying to estimate the relative velocities of the two vehicles. An indicator on his panel gave him a distance readout in meters, but he ignored it, preferring his own eyes and judgement. And slowly, slowly, the gap narrowed, the silver egg boring relentlessly through space toward him, growing larger and brighter as it came.

The Probe seemed to be ignoring his presence. That in itself was significant. Its many mechanical senses had to have long ago detected this intruder, queried the dispassionate electronic brain, received commands to execute. Possibly there was a limit beyond which no physical body could approach—and at that point the burning finger of a laser would reach out to cut him apart, or a small warhead come streaking toward the Big Bird.

There was no way of knowing. His sole defense was a laser cannon, and it was intended for offensive usage. They had not even bothered to give him training exercises in fighting off an attack.

The gap grew smaller still, and there was no reaction from the Probe. A moment later a shadow from the attach framework fell across the silvery nose. Jarl fed his maneuvering engines a bit more thrust. Before he could try another speed adjustment there was a hard bump. He cut power and put the attitude jets on automatic.

'Contact!' he said to the passive face of the flight controller, knowing it would be minutes before he would see the excitement that word generated.

Jarl took his hands off the controls, clenching and relaxing them. He suddenly realized how great the tension had been.

Jarl was too close to the rounded face of the Probe's nose to see the blue fire behind it. But the huge cloud generated enough light to brighten space beyond the shining metal horizon—and as Jarl stared, that light faded and died.

Jarl sat for a moment in stunned silence, feeling the sudden and unexpected weightlessness. Then he reported the event to Earth, just as the young controller's face lit up with excitement on hearing contact had been accomplished.

'Now that I don't need to get inside and disable the engines, what's our next move?' Jarl added. 'Have the bright boys behind the screen been working on contingency plans?'

There was nothing to do but sit and wait while the time-lag caused the curious phenomenon of instant history—all their reactions were in his past. But when the buzz of speculation died down the controller regained his professional calm. 'Jarl, it's the fast concensus here that the Probe recognized intelligent contact and turned itself off. It *wants* to be captured!—which is one of the contingencies considered here, but nobody believed it. Now they think we should start your main drive again and slow you both down without attempting to disable the engines. No one believes they will come back on.'

'No, we're going ahead with the boarding as originally planned,' a strong new voice cut in. The image of Harold Hentson appeared on the screen, a broad smile still on his face. 'The best we can manage with the Big Bird engine is to slow you both enough to pass around the sun in that tight loop. Jarl—get outside and see if there's an entry hatch you can open. Maybe we can do better.'

'And just what did you have in mind, Wild-Hair?' Jarl demanded. He had to wait an interminable time for his answer.

'The experts have all agreed you couldn't possibly understand the alien programmer well enough to command the Probe. Let's get inside and see if they're right. If they are, we lose nothing we're not prepared to lose. If they're wrong—perhaps you can save my son.'

'Do we have the time?' Jarl asked.

When the question reached Earth Harold briefly disappeared from the screen. He came back to say, 'Sure, we can spare a few hours. The trackers will tell us when the trajectory starts to get critical. Now get your butt out here and see what you can find, old man.'

'Watch how you talk to your father!' Jarl growled but obediently started unbuckling himself. Since he had never removed his spacesuit, he had only to check his oxygen supply and a few other readings before he could open the inner hatch.

This huge but cheaply designed space-going tanker-transport had a cheap airlock—and went to that small expense only because it was required to dock with the Space Station. It was a plain metal box, intruding into the pilot's compartment from the outside hatch. Both pressure doors were hand-operated, and the air inlet was a simple valve into the interior of the room, the only pressurized area on the vehicle.

Within five minutes Jarl was ready and released the inner door pressure latches. From inside the cramped airlock he operated the manual valve that swiftly bled the air into the vacuum outside. After that he opened the outer hatch and pulled himself through, twisting his body to place his feet on the metal skin. Magnetic shoes locked him in place.

The light but sturdy gridwork connecting the

two ships had plastic bumpers on the ends touching the Probe. The attitude jets kept the two craft firmly in contact. Jarl was standing inside the framework, looking at the round silver nose only meters away.

The point of entry was obvious. There was a fine line forming a circle about a meter wide, around what appeared to be the point where a line drawn through the long axis would emerge. There was a small indentation at that point.

Grasping the nearest beam, Jarl freed his feet and pulled himself along the framework to the other ship. To his pleased surprise the silver skin was weakly magnetic, at least enough that his shoes worked. He attached himself and bent over the small hole he was obviously supposed to examine.

Jarl kept up a running commentary into his suit mike as he moved. He was expecting a puzzle of some sort as the entrance examination, and was not disappointed—but it seemed so simple he wondered if it was not deceptive, and he had missed its meaning entirely.

The indentation was about four centimeters deep and as wide as the palm of his hand. Inside its perimeter was a series of round rods half a centimeter in diameter, their tops even with the metal. On each little rod was a single sharply cut line, at varying elevations and on the inside face only.

Any creature of even reasonable intelligence should recognize the circle motif, and that it was time to form a final circle. This door was not intended to be difficult.

Selecting the rod with the lowest line, Jarl pressed gently on the one to its left. With his gloves on it was difficult to move only that one, but he caught it just on the edge and succeeded. It moved easily enough. He stopped when the horizontal cut was even with that of the lowest one, and moved to the rod on the other side.

When all the rods were down a new circle had been formed, that of the aligned cuts. And their tops formed a jagged pattern—another circle, turned at an angle to the first.

A few seconds later the round plate moved slowly outward, extending directly ahead on a central shaft. When it stopped, the door was its own width from the main body.

A light came on inside.

Jarl pulled himself over the curving edge and into the hole. No creature much larger, and wearing a spacesuit, could have made it between the round edge and the immovable extended shaft.

He was in a cylinder of open space, two meters wide and five deep. The shaft ran its full length, emerging from the rear wall. A line of metal rods five centimeters wide and fifteen long wound around the shaft in a regular pattern from one end to the other.

Jarl grasped a rod and pulled himself along the shaft. As his hands moved his eyes were trying to comprehend what they saw on the concave surface on all sides. Some of it seemed to make sense, to form a possibly understandable pattern. But much of the alien equipment he could have reached and touched failed to register properly. His sight could absorb the details, but not his brain.

When he was almost to the rear wall a round section of blank plate to his left warmed to a dusky red, then faded into shades of pale violet.

Jarl had been talking continuously into his mike, without giving the controller a chance to answer.

Since the nose hatch was still open his signal should be reaching the Big Bird, and from there going to Earth.

The violet-tinted plate extended itself slightly from the wall. Streaks of color circled around the perimeter, whirled, broke—and an image formed.

Jarl was looking down the length of the cylinder he was in. It did not show him there, which meant this was a recording. As he watched, the view began to move along the shaft, until it seemed to reach his present position. It turned toward the wall to Jarl's back. Then he felt a slight vibration of metal and swung around. A larger section of wall had moved out and tilted downward, within arm's reach.

There was a seat of sorts attached to the curved plate, at a lower elevation. Jarl seated himself in it, glancing quickly at the inevitable series of rods extending upward above the plate's convex surface. Three red screens had erected themselves at the far end and were swiftly warming up to violet.

Jarl turned back to the main show, where an image of the controls he was facing had appeared. And, finally, he saw one of the builders of this automated marvel.

A creature appeared from the side and seated itself in the chair Jarl was occupying. It was humanoid in form but with a body composed of a series of circles. The trunk was wide-hipped and narrow-shouldered, the belly fat and round. The head was shaped like a billiard ball, hairless, with a wide mouth upturned in a perpetual smile. It had ears, but they were flattened against the bald skull. There were two recessed eyes above the mouth, but no nose or nostril slits that Jarl could see.

The humanoid wore a loose-fitting gown that

hung almost to its knees; these scenes had been shot in a gravity environment. The two legs beneath the gown were short and sturdy and well bowed. The bare arms looked muscular and strong.

Judging by its height in the chair, the humanoid could have been only about a meter tall. But its bulk was so wide and stout it would have equalled a human in weight. The closest Jarl could come to classifying it in Earthly terms was as a very sturdy gnome, or human dwarf. He decided to think of it as a gnome.

The alien extended an arm and clamped a broad hand around the left rod in the line closest to the chair. He pressed down—and the scene shifted without warning or fading to an exterior view of the silver Probe. The engines were off. But as Jarl watched, blue flames spurted from both and swiftly increased to a huge, fire-shot cloud.

Just as abruptly, the scene returned to the interior, showing the gnome's hand on the rod. He lifted it back to the top of its travel—and the fast scene change came again, showing the engine fire fading away.

Jarl turned quickly from the screen to the real control board. That left hand rod was in the up position.

So you started the engines just by pressing one round rod to the bottom. Simple enough. Like the entrance 'puzzle', it was not meant to be difficult. Some of the others must be attitude jets and internal ship controls. But how did you steer this thing? And what did you use for orientation and guidance?

In a step-by-step, logical, orderly sequence, the

screen proceeded to teach him.

The alien thought patterns were not really that difficult to understand. The major item that seemed to distinguish them from the human was that evidently they did not use identification symbols on their controls. Every rod had a separate function, and together they formed an easy-to-operate manual control system—if you could remember what each one did. Since there were over twenty of them, it wasn't easy.

Jarl settled down to learning how to operate his second new ship within a week.

He had one lucky break. When the gnome at the controls had run through an entire operational sequence, he touched a final rod that controlled the instruction screen itself. He depressed it only slightly, then immediately raised it. The screen faded back into red patterns, but warmed to light violet again—and the instructional film started repeating itself.

Jarl avoided touching the lever that could change the program. He had a great deal to learn here.

* * *

'Hal?' The speaker was Wilson, the launch conductor. 'That federal marshall is on the visiphone. He wants to know when you're coming back to the Tower.'

Harold glanced at his watch, startled. It was past 12:00. He had become so absorbed in listening to Jarl's steady reporting he had not realized how the time was passing.

Harold stood up, stretching muscle cramped from sitting almost motionless for two hours. The TV camera on the front of Jarl's ship was sending back an unchanging view of the nose of the Probe, with its round hatch extended almost a meter toward the attached intercepter. But though they had only Jarl's verbal description to go on, the drama that had unfolded inside that odd door had kept them glued in their seats.

'I'd better go on to jail, or McDougal is going to die of apoplexy. Wilson—will there be any problem transferring enough oxygen from the Big Bird over to the Probe to last for two weeks? Pete—' Dawson was sitting at the next console '—do we still need to loop around the sun? If so, can we move out to a safe distance, using the Probe's engines, and still get back here within the two weeks? We want Jarl back alive and the Probe slowed enough to enter Earth orbit. Is that possible?'

Peter Dawson had obviously been mentally working the problem as they waited. Logical and orderly as always, he laid it out for them. 'Hal, we still have to go around the sun. It's already too close to turn now without going well inside the orbit of Mercury, and facing unacceptable heat. Our safest bet is to go ahead and fire the Bird's engines for the four hours we have left, discard it, and make our final calculations on the retrograde decel of which we know the Probe is capable. I'd say we can keep it at least sixty million klicks from the sun, at a rough guess, and get it back here within two weeks by constant use of the Probe's engines.'

Wilson had been waiting to speak. 'Hal, the extra oxygen was installed in a separate tank, which Jarl can easily move to the Probe. But unless he can close that hatch and have an air-tight room, he may have to stay in his spacesuit the whole two weeks.'

'Any reason he can't live in the suit?'

'It would be damned uncomfortable, and he couldn't eat. We can add water to the suit-tank with it pressurized, though, so he could survive.'

'Why don't we plan for the best possible answers and accept less when it happens. Pete, I want you to take full charge of this mission until I'm out of jail. With luck, Fred Buck will have me free by to-night. Get Jarl to transfer food and water as well as the oxygen after he fires his engines. If he can close that hatch he could release just a little gas and wait to see if the pressure in the Probe stabilizes. Before he does that, in fact the first thing we should ask of him is to move a camera over. Call out the rest of our science lab staff and let them have a look in-side. Put them all on standby here for consultation. Get opinions as to whether releasing oxygen into the Probe might cause an explosion or any other damage. In short, carry on.'

Pete looked a little stunned. He had just been handed a responsibility he apparently did not want. But he nodded and turned to his console vis-iphone.

Harold decided to drive. Before 1:00 he was pull-ing into his parking slot at RI Headquarters. He found McDougal sitting in the president's office, eyes still locked on the desk screen Pat Pajick had tied in for him. The marshall seemed well aware he was the only non-RI employee fortunate enough to be watching history in the making.

Pat Pajick had hurried inside behind Harold. 'Fred Buck left a few minutes ago for Orlando. He's going to try to have the paperwork filed by the time you get there. If the Judge won't release you on bond—and he may not, for a severe contempt citation—Fred will take it immediately to the senior jurist on the federal court of appeals.'

'Just so he has me out by dark. And see if you can arrange to have a visiphone installed in my cell, if I wind up in one, and pipe in the show. In fact it's probably time we contacted the Tri–D networks, let 'em in on it. They can carry it as a news event; no sponsorship. Tell them . . .' Harold stopped. He was about to get involved in a whole new area, and this was not the time for it. 'Hell, put out an all-points visibull. Pete Dawson is in charge of RI until I return. Take it up with him.'

McDougal reluctantly rose from Harold's chair and the steady view of the Probe's nose. Jarl was almost ready to fire his ship's engines. The officer looked at Harold with new respect. 'Well, Mr. Hentson, it looks like your crazy idea wasn't so bad after all. If this works out, I guess you won't spend much time in jail.'

Harold clapped him on the shoulder. 'Maybe not even long enough to catch a nap. But let's get going, before that tough judge has you in there with me for being so slow.'

'Yessir, we had better be moving all right, before the afternoon traffic starts.'

Harold left for his second confinement in three days, in a cheerful frame of mind. From here on, always assuming Jarl's mind held up and the Probe was ultimately captured, it should be a downhill slide to home.

13

Monday, June 13, 2011

'Hey Jodie!' Strobe sounded excited. 'Al Murray just broke in to say God Hentson captured the Probe and is about to go aboard and fly it back! RI is going to furnish WWN live coverage from space. Want to watch?'

Jodie reluctantly sat up in bed and yawned. She had been taking a late afternoon nap, having gotten little sleep on Sunday night. She wondered how Jesus Hentson felt. Probably good, if his father had actually intercepted Probe.

The program was on the Tri-D set but being broadcast flat. And the audio link between Jarl and KSC was not being relayed. Instead, Alfred Murray was keeping up a running commentary.

'Fellow world citizens, that's Jarl Hentson you see moving toward the Probe, carrying his supply of frozen food. We're told he's already transferred all the bottled oxygen he has, and the water. They thought of bringing over a radio, but that wasn't practical, and his suit radio won't reach this far. When the two vehicles separate we're going to lose contact with him, unless the Probe has a radio and he can learn how to operate it. He claims to have already learned how to fly this strange visitor.'

Jodie saw Jarl wriggle over the edge of the outthrust door and disappear. 'As we understand it,' Murray went on, 'RI now says the Probe was *meant* to be captured, and Hal Hentson, president of RI, was right all along. He's in jail in Orlando, Florida, by the way, on a federal contempt charge. Now Jarl Hentson, who is Harold Hentson's son—and also his father, according to what we hear, but we're not supposed to talk about that—has a camera set up inside the Probe, and RI has promised us a look before they separate and the camera loses power. After that—hold it! Here's the RI acting president with some words for us.'

The view did not change, but a new, somewhat halting voice replaced Murray's. 'Fellow citizens, uh . . .' Dawson was evidently aware of the size of his audience and was bothered by it. 'We are, uh . . . almost ready to separate the ships. We're going to switch you to our second channel, for a view inside the Probe. It's a—a little hard to understand, some of it.' As he spoke the static scene of the Probe's nose abruptly vanished, to be replaced by an inside view of an apparently long cylinder. It was like peering into the interior of a barrel, except that the walls contained hundreds of items of equipment, some of it of incomprehensible purpose. Jarl Hentson was stuffing cartons of frozen food into an opening behind what appeared to be a solid block of red steel. He locked them in place with tape.

'Our power system is not . . . well, compatible with theirs, and we can't operate the camera except on a cord from our own ship,' Dawson went on. 'We'll switch to the outside camera and let you watch Mr. Jarl Hentson fire up the Probe's engines, but when he pulls away, that will be it until the Probe returns to Earth. Just a few minutes more and I think he'll be ready.'

Dawson fell silent, and the wrinkled but somehow ageless face of Alfred Murray briefly appeared, before the exterior camera view returned. Jodie and Strobe watched for almost an hour. They saw the Big Bird disengage from the Probe and retreat and lower itself. The Probe remained on camera. Two of Strobe's friends entered and silently joined them in front of the set. Finally they saw the Probe's engines come to life and watched the silver stranger move ahead and abruptly out of camera view. The fatherly visage of Murray returned, to tell the world the worst was over, and with luck they would have the captured ship orbiting the Earth within two weeks. And he mentioned again that Harold Hentson, whose daring and imagination had made this extraordinary scientific adventure possible, was residing in an Orlando federal cell.

'But he won't be for long,' said Strobe, rising and turning off the set.

'Sarcoma . . .' it was Diana Sharp, the lushly pretty black-haired Latin girl who for a time had been Harold Hentson's lover. Do you really think . . . I mean, did we do the right thing? Not that it mattered in the end, but . . .'

Jodie let surprise show on her face. 'Why of course we did! And the fact we lost one battle doesn't mean the war is over. We can get our lawyer to file a petition as a friend of the court—*amicus curae* I think they call it—to get Jesus Hentson sentenced for a few months on that contempt charge. We can organize a protest at WorldGov in

Geneva—in fact that will be my next job—to demand the Probe be sent on its way again after they get it back here. What right did we have to interfere with it anyway? We can suggest they take God Hentson off first, for humanitarian reasons. Our basic thrust can be that MoonEye and the Space Station and all the rest already take up far too much of resources, and trying to learn a new way of powering a rocket by studying the Probe will be just throwing good money after bad. Why do we *need* more powerful rocket engines? We've explored the whole solar system with unmanned spacecraft and landed that crew on Mars. What has it all gotten us? Absolutely nothing! We shouldn't have any real problem convincing WorldGov we can't afford the billions it would take to understand and develop the technology on that thing. Besides, what if its owners come after it someday?'

'RI is claiming it was *supposed* to be captured!' Diana reminded Jodie, her voice a little high. 'That's why it had the manual controls and everything. Before I came over here I heard a commentator saying a Space Benefits scientist says it will almost certainly have some kind of message on board, telling us how to contact the builders by radio. We won't *have* to actually fly to their home star! It will take years and years each way, but he says that once we know where to point our largest radio telescopes, we can send and receive information. After we learn each other's language, that is. And maybe there's some sort of book or something on the Probe that will even tell us that!'

Jodie stared at Diana, her face cold. 'There are all kinds of "maybes". Maybe it will have a better liquor-making machine inside, and we can all get drunk! But we know for sure that if Space Benefits funds anything of the kind, the money will be spent on hardware and not on *people!* The real point is that we have too much technology *now!* Let's don't make the situation worse by adding a whole new batch before we learn to use what we have.'

Diana rose to her feet. 'I think I'll be going. I don't agree with what you're doing, and I don't want to help any more. In fact I'd apologize to Hal Hentson for fingering him, except that he doesn't know I did it, and he got away from you anyway. I joined FOE because I believed in its goals, Sarcoma. But you've turned those into something senseless and sick! Oh, don't look so shocked and worried, I won't tell anything I know. I don't want to join Hal in jail!' And she hurried out.

Jodie stared at the closing door with somber eyes. This defeat was more serious than she liked to admit. Diana might have been influenced by the fact she was obviously still in love with Jesus Hentson—but a lot of people were going to share her views. Which made going to Geneva and stirring up the FOE chapter there all the more urgent. Two weeks' advance work should be enough to ensure a really massive turn-out. The Hentsons could still be stopped.

Hal's face swam into her mind, and for a moment she was drawn back into their long night together. She felt a pleasant stir of warmth at the base of her spine. It was odd that he could be such a considerate, gently fierce man as a lover, and yet have so little regard for people as a whole. But perhaps that was one of the dichotomies possible when one had a closed mind.

'Care to take a couple of weeks off and go with me to Geneva, Strobe?' Jodie asked.

'Me? Migod, Sarcoma, I can't afford it! I've used my leave for the year, and I don't have the money anyway. We have Jan Stugart there, she can do more for you than I could anyway.'

'Probably so,' said Jodie, rising and heading for her bedroom. She still felt somewhat tired and listless. 'I'll pack in the morning. Give my regards to the chapter at the next meeting and tell them it was a job well done, regardless. Next time we'll cut the Hentsons and SB down to size.'

'Yeah. Next time,' said Strobe dutifully.

* * *

Jarl sat in the oddly curved seat, facing the front of the closed room. The large screen on which the operational instructions endlessly repeated themselves was to his right, the three screens which were a part of the control mechanism directly ahead, behind the banks of rods. He had closed the entry hatch before activating the engines. With the Probe in motion he felt a comforting weight again, though it seemed less than half a G. His back was pressed against the set firmly enough that he felt its different curvature as uncomfortable. But it was something he could easily endure.

He glanced at the external pressure gauge on the arm of his suit. It was registering almost half a kilogram. He had just turned off the valve on the oxygen tank, and the big question now was whether the pressure would hold. If it did, he could release enough more to build up to two kilograms. That was a thin atmosphere but breathable when it was pure oxygen.

Jarl had tried peering behind the various extended panels in the curving walls to see if there were openings to the huge spherical interior. If there were, he had not been able to spot them. As with the outer walls, the inside surfaces that he could see were a maze of equipment.

The three screens on the front of the convex control panel were from three exterior cameras. He had not yet discovered any means of viewing the interior of the Probe. The center camera showed nothing but a swirling cloud of blue fire, streaming constantly backward. It was obviously mounted near the engines. The other two were front-mounted, widely apart on each side. They showed star fields ahead. And by swiveling the one on the left, he could see the sun.

The controllers on Earth had used the thrust left in the Big Bird to change his velocity, but not the direction. Before cutting off the TV they had fed him a complete flight plan, once convinced he could actually guide the Probe. At that moment he was still decelerating. When he stopped the engines after one hundred and ninety-six minutes, he would be in a flight path that would take him just outside the orbit of Venus. Once past the sun he was to ignite the engines again, and actually accelerate for four days. That was the maximum added velocity the Probe was capable of shedding before reaching Earth and took nine days off the time the wider orbit around the sun would have otherwise required. Then there would be seven straight days of deceleration toward Earth. They had not been able to compute his exact arrival velocity but felt certain it would be slow enough to put him into an elliptical Earth orbit.

Jarl glanced at his watch again and saw that less

than three minutes had passed. His gauge still read half a kilo, but that meant nothing over such a short period of time. He could only hope this odd little control cylinder was as isolated as it appeared, and that it would hold oxygen. He was already feeling uncomfortable and tired of the heavy spacesuit.

At the end of an hour the external gauge read exactly what it had before. So the area was tight, at least up to that pressure. He was going to quadruple it, and there was always the possibility something might give. If it did, and all the air escaped, he would soon be dead.

Jarl hesitated. Did he have the right to risk his life? He could assume the gnomes had anticipated this need and deliberately arranged for the little cylinder to hold whatever gas mixture a visitor needed. Which meant the rods, screens, and all other surfaces were made of extremely passive materials, to avoid reactions with corrosive gases—such as oxygen.

On the other hand, he could be guilty of anthropomorphizing.

Despite that possibility, Jarl would have been willing to bet the gnomes were oxygen breathers. There were more similarities than differences between them and humans, at the macroscopic level. What a micro-biological exam might show was anybody's guess. If they were as thoughtful and careful in their preparations as it appeared, this little room would hold almost any atmosphere, and he could unsuit in perfect safety.

And if he was wrong and some fragile panel sprang a leak under two kilos of pressure, the Probe would not be captured. There was no way of predicting what its program required after an intelligent entity had entered the manual control chamber. But it was not likely to reverse course and land itself on the last planet scanned.

Which threw him right back to the beginning. Was he convinced he understood the alien thought processes well enough to risk it?

Jarl decided he was. He opened the manual valve on the oxygen tank to maximum and waited. When the pressure reached two kilos he turned it off and unsuited. There was no use in waiting for stabilization. At this point he had either won or lost.

It felt good to be outside the confining suit. It felt even better, after about an hour, when the pressure had stabilized at just below two kilos, and there had been no reaction from the visible equipment or the inside of the Probe.

There was nothing more to do while waiting for the time to cut off the engines. And he felt reasonably confident he could operate the control rods from memory now if he had to. Jarl reached for the one he had been warned would change or stop the repeating program. He depressed it and watched the fat gnome fade from view on the large screen. With the rod at the bottom of its travel, he rotated it to the left—and a new program appeared. Again without introduction or sound, it started playing across the concave round surface.

This story began with the Probe in orbit around a large, reddish-colored world, hulking huge in the background. The Probe was apparently complete, ready to depart. But then it began disintegrating, breaking into component parts. Small ships of a totally different design appeared and began taking each component back to the surface. And then Jarl realized these people presented history from present to past, not in chronological forward order as was the human custom, and settled down to learn.

* *

Monday, June 27, 2011

'It's one after four; let's go,' said Sanderson. He led the way out of the thick brush toward the tall fence, carrying a collapsible ladder. Jodie followed, after looking carefully around. The bearded young guidance engineer had assured her the man on duty inside the Launch Control Center was a FOE member, and they would be seen on monitoring screens but not reported. The guards on patrol were not and had to be avoided.

Sanderson set the ladder against the overhanging fence and hastily climbed up. He crouched on one of the supports that extended the barbed wire a meter outward, and waited for Jodie. When she joined him, he lifted the ladder and let it down on the inside. Two minutes later they were safely on the ground, the ladder folded up and hidden under a prominent bush.

The launch pad was almost deserted at this early hour, only a few technicians performing some last-minute operations. The Big Bird was sitting silently on its stand; liftoff was at 11:37. Jodie and Keith Sanderson were wearing the standard technician's white coveralls, and it was unlikely they would be challenged once safely inside.

They took the elevator up to the White Room on the top of the Swing Arm leading from the Launch Tower to the vehicle, seeing no one along the way. A short, stout woman with her hair tucked under a white cap was working on a TV camera mounted to face the door. She looked curiously at them, particularly at Jodie's unconfined red hair, but made no comment when Sanderson confidently led the way through the little room and on through a cramped airlock into the pilot's compartment. Jodie realized she should have tucked her red wig under a net. It was the only part of her Sarcoma costume she had been able to wear.

Once they were out of hearing Jodie asked, 'Won't she report us?'

'Not likely. She's just here to repair that camera. She'll think we left after she did.'

Sanderson knelt at the left rear of the pilot's console and undid the fasteners on a plate in the wall. When it came off, Jodie saw a cabletray loaded with thick black wires. At the rear of the compartments the cables and tray exited through airtight grommets, all carefully sealed with bolted guards.

Jodie turned to face the pilot's console, knelt, and worked her way in backward on top of the tray. When she lay flat against the side wall there was just room enough left for Sanderson. He joined her, then attached a large magnet with a handgrip to the steel plate and lifted it into position. She held a handlight for him, and he sealed it around the edges with a strap of adhesive.

'We'll have to be quiet when the pilot enters, but till then we can talk in whispers,' Sanderson said in a low voice. 'And it may get a little stuffy, but as I said last night, we should get enough oxygen through the adjoining cable cutouts. Now we have to hope no one notices those bare bolts on the outside of the plate.'

They were crowded uncomfortably close together. There was no way to separate their bodies when both lay on their stomachs. Jodie turned on her right side, facing Sanderson, and managed to obtain a few centimeters of welcome space. He was a reasonably attractive man, but she disliked forced physical contact with anyone, male or female.

'This is going to be a hell of an uncomfortable seven hours,' Jodie whispered.

'There's no help for it. Why don't you go to sleep, if you can. You must be out on your feet, after flying in from Geneva yesterday afternoon.'

'I *am* tired,' Jodie admitted. She had been on the go almost constantly in Switzerland, trying hard to work up a successful demonstration. The actual performance had been a dismal flop, and World-Gov officials had apparently ignored them. The whole world seemed to have been intrigued by the dramatic way God Hentson had captured the Probe, and the fact he had successfully taken it around the sun and was again approaching Earth. Even the strongest supporters of FOE in Geneva had been apathetic, apparently certain they had no chance of convincing the world the Probe should be released.

Despite the hardness of the cables, Jodie did doze off. She awoke several hours later to find Keith Sanderson peacefully asleep beside her. She placed an ear against the entrance panel; all was silent inside the pilot's compartment. It was almost 9:00 by her luminous watch dial. She needed to urinate but not so strongly that she could not sleep again. When she awoke the next time it was to feel a hand over her mouth and Sanderson's face at her ear. 'S-h-h-h! The pilot is inside, and we'll be lifting off in thirty minutes.'

Her bladder was so full Jodie was distinctly uncomfortable. She resigned herself to wait in patience. And somehow the time passed, and eventually the muted thunder of a giant engine filled the little compartment with a vibrating rumble of sound. When the big vehicle lifted off it felt to Jodie as if the entire monstrous thing was falling apart. She could not help remembering this was a cheaply made rocket, designed to be discarded after use. A Big Bird was guided back into the atmosphere after unloading its cargo at the Space Station, the burned remnants falling into some deserted part of an ocean. The pilot returned on the next Earth-bound Space Shuttle, which could land like an airplane.

It was twelve minutes before the sound of a rocket firing suddenly ceased. Sanderson immediately began pulling the tape off the hatch. When it was clear, he seized the grip on his magnet and eased the plate forward and off the bolts. He held it with one hand and pulled himself easily out with the other. Sanderson had been in space twice before, on trips to the Space Station.

Jodie followed the young engineer. It was easy to pull yourself along flat, but she bumped the edge of the wall with one hip, hurting herself. She straightened up outside, clinging to the nearest solid projection and forcing her feet to the floor. The pilot had turned in his chair and was watching in amazement, having just looked that way and spotted Sanderson.

The pilot began speaking rapidly into his spacesuit microphone. Jodie unzipped one coverall pocket and drew her small pistol. She pointed it at the pilot and gestured for him to be silent. She saw his lips stop moving; he had already reported their presence. She waved the gun and said aloud, 'Take off the helmet, mister.'

For short missions such as this the pilot normally remained suited, although his compartment was filled with air. Slowly he lifted his hands and obeyed. Sanderson moved to assist him, and a minute later the helmet came off and was stuffed into a drawer.

'Just who the hell are you, and what do you think you're doing?' the pilot demanded the instant they could hear him.

Jodie smiled sweetly at him. 'Just call me Sarcoma. My friend is Ken. And what we are doing is very simple. We are going to meet the Probe, get Jarl Hentson off, and send it on its merry way. You are going to help us.'

'The hell I am!'

Jodie lifted the gun and took careful aim. 'You are going to do as we say, or I'll shoot you here and now. Ken can operate this rocket, if he has to. You are highly expendable, mister. Either you give me your word you'll cooperate, and we all make it back to the Space Station—or I kill and we try it on our own. Which is it to be?'

The pilot gave her a long, level look, obviously trying to see if she was bluffing. Jodie waited, the gun never wavering. Then the astronaut saw the flight controller on his small screen, who was frantically gesturing, and absently reached to flip a switch on his console, Jodie almost pulled the trigger before she realized what he was doing.

'Denbow! What do those people want? Let us talk to them!'

'Turn him off,' Jodie ordered.

Denbow looked at her again, decided she was

not bluffing, and turned the viewscreen completely off.

'I have a program already worked out for the intercept,' Sanderson said, producing a disk from his pocket. 'I'm no astronaut, but I can handle the local maneuvering for the actual contact. We'll make it, with or without you.'

Denbow shrugged, and turned back to his console. 'Okay, you've convinced me. But I still think you're crazy. You'll just smash us into the Probe.'

'This flight plan was carefully worked out. We have enough propellants on board to go about four million klicks out, turn around, and match velocities with the Probe as it comes in. After we get God Hentson off, we'll disable its engines. It will miss Earth by a considerable margin, while we decelerate to rendezvous with Earth and the Space Station.'

'And there isn't another rocket on Earth capable of catching the Probe,' Jodie added. 'The next Big Bird can't fly in less than a week.'

'So you actually think you can deprive Earth of the Probe, eh? Oh yeah, I remember you. I saw you on the Tri–D when you led that bunch of nuts who tried to stop the launch. Well, you didn't suceed then and you won't now!'

'Suppose you just feed the new program into the flight computer and let us worry about that,' said Sanderson, his voice trying hard to be tough and mean; it didn't succeed. But Denbow glanced at Jodie, shrugged, and did as he was told.

14

Monday, June 22, 2011

'That is absolutely incredible!' said Harold Hent-son.

Pat Pajick grimaced. 'It's true, Hal. Wilson just called me. Somehow two of those FOE fanatics managed to stow away on the monthly supply flight. Our ground controllers got a good look at them before the screen went blank. The wom-an was the red-haired witch who calls herself Sarcoma.'

Harold's visicon trilled. 'What is it?' he asked the gray-haired secretary on his screen.

'Hal, we just got a weirdo call, someone who wouldn't identify herself. She said Alfred Murray will be on WWN any minute now with something you should hear.'

'Okay, thanks Marge. We'll tune him in.'

Harold elevated his desk Tri–D screen and ac-tivated the news channel. Two minutes later they were listening to the sonorous voice of Alfred Mur-ray, reading from a statement supplied to WWN by Sarcoma. It was a declaration of intent to in-tercept the Probe, illegally seized in deep space by the Rockets International Corporation, remove the mentally retarded son of RI president Hal Hentson, and return him safely to Earth. The Probe would be left with enough velocity to take it on out of the solar system. Mankind would be saved from another unconscionable attempt by the aerospace lobby to pour more WorldGov billions into useless and unneeded space technology.

'Who let those two get on board the rocket?' Harold demanded when the newscast ended.

'No one knows, Hal. The guard on the monitor screens last night saw nothing unusual. A technician working in the White Room saw them enter, but she had no way of knowing they were unauthorized. The man with Sarcoma has to be one of our people, someone with access to the flight plans. I'll have security get a description from the controllers and track him down.'

'Good. And when this is over, Pat, we're going to have a little house-cleaning at RI. I want security checks run on all our people in launch operations, from the janitors to the VPs. Anyone who belongs to one of the organizations opposing the space program is due for a transfer. We won't fire a person for association-by-conviction off the job —that would be illegal anyway—but we can get them out of the sensitive positions.'

'We can try,' said Pat.

'Dammit, I feel so *helpless!* Isn't there anything whatever we can do? What does Raoul Stone say about the possibility of taking charge with ground controls? Can we turn them around from here?'

'Wilson says no chance. That vehicle is controlled entirely by its self-contained flight program. And somehow they made up a new one that gave them the trajectory they wanted. Probably used our equipment to do it—and on company time.'

'Then I guess we sit and wait,' said Harold, the unusual feeling of helplessness growing stronger. He had felt this way in jail, for the three days it had taken Fred Buck to get him released.

The confinement had been a strange, unnerving experience, far worse than the single day Harold had spent locked in the FOE prison apartment. There he had felt in charge of his own fate, been fighting his own battle. In the federal jail he had had no choice but to depend on Fred Buck and his staff. The thought that he might conceivably spend months behind bars had deeply troubled Harold, left him worried and sleepless at night. Again and again he had retraced the steps that had gotten him there, considering and analyzing the paths he had not taken. And in the end he could see no other way. His decision to intercept the Probe had been the right one. Pressing the launch sequencer switch himself had been the only way to clear innocent RI employees of possible contempt charges. The fact his act had made him seem deliberately contemptuous of the judge was his personal burden.

Harold had gone behind bars expecting to be out before dark. Instead, the Judge had sentenced him to a month in jail, suspended except for three days. Only Jarl's success in space had kept Harold from serving a year. And now that triumph could be ruined by two fanatics who were risking their lives to stop the Probe.

Two fanatics . . . as he and his RI associates were also fanatics, on the opposite side. Harold was convinced of the rightness of his cause, but so were the FOE people and their allies. Somehow there had to be a meeting of minds, a better understanding of what was actually best for humanity. The fine work the environmentalists had performed in cleaning the nation's air and streams should not be lost in mindless attacks against all science and technology.

'Hal, the two hijackers still have to deal with Jarl Hentson,' Pat Pajick reminded him. 'He won't be an easy man to stop.'

* * *

But Jarl felt that he had been almost stopped already. He was having severe difficulty retaining his mental faculties well enough to operate the Probe.

It was a peculiar, disagreeable sensation. He would be studying one of the historical pictorial records when his mind would start to drift. Sometimes it was memories of childhood, obviously his own. On other occasions he saw dim, cloudy pictures of objects he could not identify. Sometimes there were memories of toys he had never had and places he had never seen. Often Lily's face swam before his eyes, frequently that of Hal, and somewhat more often, that of Robert Brown. Feelings came with each face, one of warmth and love for Lily, of love mingled with wariness for Hal, of placid acceptance with Robert.

He would arouse from such gently intruding reveries to find a large portion of some recording had passed unnoticed and was forgotten. Then for a moment he would be himself again and realize that his grasp of external reality was rapidly fading. Internally, there was no clear distinction between his mind and that of young Jarl, no fight for consciousness nor control. In a way beyond his understanding, some characteristics of both were melding, blending, becoming one.

Jarl wondered what the final result would be.

In the meantime he had little to do but wait. The Probe's engines were firing and would continue to do so until it entered a highly elliptical Earth orbit. He could already see his home world, a small blue ball in the distance, one growing slowly but steadily larger. His only remaining vital task was to cut off the Probe's engines at the right time. As best he could judge by vision alone, the Probe was on the flight path selected for it. In two more days he would be home.

Or at least what was left of him would.

Regardless, they had saved the Probe. Assuming he retained enough sense to press the right rod at the right time, the Probe and all its marvelous knowledge belonged to Mankind. Wild-Hair Harold had been right after all, and when it counted most. And what a prize this visitor was! Jarl had spent many hours studying the extensive visual records, there being little else to do, and grew more impressed with each new showing. Early in the program a friendly gnome had presented an intricate diagram of star positions, one that would obviously tell an astronomer the home location; it meant little to Jarl. There was a simplified diagram of what was apparently a hyperfine transition between parallel and anti-parallel proton and electron spins of the hydrogen atom. He saw a tiny flash of radiation emerge. Jarl felt certain the wavelength would be 21 centimeters, the most likely 'universal signal'. So 1,420 Megahertz was the frequency on which to try interstellar communications, as had long been suspected. The gnomes had not only shown the location of their home but had indicated the frequency on which they would be listening for calls.

There was more, so incredibly much more. Earth's best brains would be busy for years trying to understand it. And the waiting treasures were not restricted to physicists, or even engineers and other technologists. There was a wealth of data in historical records, plus a possible quantum jump in Man's knowledge of intelligence and its manifestations—the latter made possible through the study of a completely alien species and its society. New patterns of thought would emerge, different and original concepts. Even—Jarl laughed aloud, though there was no one to hear—new religious beliefs, an altered perspective on Man's place in the larger universe. The easily impressionable people who had tried to stop the launch might, a few years from now, be in the forefront of some new movement, dedicated to ceremonies worshipful of the all-wise aliens.

Jarl laughed again, and dozed off where he sat, and awoke some time later with his mind dim and his percepts confused. Mama had been gone for a long time. He wished Hal would come in to see him. Without actually formulating the thought in words, he wondered if Robert loved him. At times he seemed to, but at others, he was distant and remote, playing games and talking while his mind was obviously elsewhere. He wondered why Robert didn't love him as much as Mama and Hal did.

* * *

Tuesday, June 28, 2011

'There it is,' said Denbow.

Jodie looked ahead and up through the forward window. She saw a silvery ovoid, tiny at this distance, suspended on a larger cloud of blue fire.

The Big Bird had been firing steadily for over seven hours, and despite the fact she had spent more time in the co-pilot's chair than Sanderson, she was bone-deep tired. The times the extra person had to sit flat on the floor with legs extended were the worst.

On the trip out, Sanderson had thoughtfully built two rest periods into the flight plan. This long return burn, to counteract the velocity they had acquired and match the forward speed of the Probe, was an unrelieved grind. But now the target was in sight, and they still had more than enough propellants to decelerate and enter Earth orbit.

Denbow turned off the main drive and started closing by sight, using the maneuvering engines. Their velocity barely exceeded that of the Probe. Since the other spaceship was still decelerating, he could hold the Big Bird in front of the Probe and the two would eventually meet—but it was faster to use power.

'What makes you think Jarl Hentson will let you inside?' Denbow asked Jodie, as the Probe seemed to drift down and closer in their sight.

'He's been out of touch since he closed that round hatch in the nose. I'm sure he'll think Sanderson is an astronaut, sent up here to tell him something he has to know. Why else would RI waste another Big Bird? We're hoping he'll turn off the engines, to make the contact easier. Since he'll have put his spacesuit back on before he can open the hatch, all we should have to do is force him to transfer over here. The Probe will then miss Earth by a half-million kilometers and keep on going right out of the solar system.'

'Did you think we came this far without working

it out?' asked Sanderson, his voice somewhat squeaky over the radio. He was dressed in a spacesuit, with his radio jack plugged into the ship's intercom.

'It wouldn't have surprised me a bit,' said Denbow, obvious contempt in his voice.

'I'm a guidance engineer, mister. I helped write the program you started with and did the one that got us here by myself. We know what we're doing.'

'I doubt that,' said Denbow. He glanced at Jodie, who was standing with her feet braced against the floor, her back to the frame of the airlock. There was less than one G holding her in position. She had traveled extensively, but this was her first venture into space. And while she had not experienced the stomach cramps nor the indigestion that bothered many first-time travelers, she had suffered badly from a sense of disorientation. At the moment her weight said the vertical bulkhead was the floor, while her eyes said otherwise. So far, she had managed adequately by ignoring the pull of acceleration and keeping her body physically upright in relation to the floor.

Jodie was still holding her pistol. She or Sanderson had kept Denbow under constant watch since they emerged from hiding. So far he had had the good sense not to try anything foolish.

'You'd better hope we know, Denbow,' Jodie said, making her voice cold and hard. 'We're a bunch of nutty fanatics, remember? If we can't get Jarl Hentson off and return to Earth, we might just ram into the Probe and destroy both vehicles.'

Denbow looked down at his console. 'The thought that you would is why I've gone along so far. I could never see myself as a martyr.'

'Then you aren't an entirely hopeless case. Come to the next Orlando FOE meeting after we get back. You'll be our first astronaut member.'

Denbow was silent. They were now almost on the same flight path as the Probe and moving rapidly closer. When they were within a few thousand meters, the great blue cloud behind it abruptly flickered out.

'See! We told you!' Jodie cried aloud in delight. 'God Hentson shut his engines down. What do you want to bet he'll let Sanderson inside? It's all over but the shouting!'

Denbow abruptly cut his own power. They were now rapidly closing the gap; he had to put his maneuvering engines on full reverse thrust. Within minutes they were approaching the silver nose. They stopped, in relation to the Probe, only meters away.

Jodie saw that Denbow was sweating slightly, and his face was pink. She had a sinking feeling that a disaster had narrowly been averted, that if it had been Sanderson at the console their mission would have ended seconds later when they smashed into the shining metal egg.

Which might have accomplished the objective, but was hardly what Jodie wanted. Like the astronaut, she had no desire to be a martyr. This interception was Keith Sanderson's idea. If she had not believed him when he said it could be done safely, she would not have come along.

As it was, they would undoubtedly be captured, and her true identity as Judy Karlson exposed. She might even have to go to prison for commandeering the Big Bird. The attorney in the Orlando FOE chapter has assured her there was little SB could do to them for detouring the Probe. There was no registered owner to file a complaint.

'Are you ready?' Jodie asked Sanderson. The bearded young engineer nodded and unstrapped himself from the co-pilot's chair. He attempted to rise and floundered helplessly for a moment before regaining his equilibrium. Jodie was still braced against the bulkhead and in control of her movements. She watched Denbow while Sanderson was momentarily helpless, but the astronaut made no hostile move.

Sanderson got himself oriented and pushed off toward the tiny airlock. He managed to get inside without further problems and closed the inner hatch.

'Denbow, I want you to know—I want you to *believe!*—that I will shoot if you try anything that could get him hurt. I don't know what you're doing there—but if Sanderson doesn't appear in front of us in just a few minutes, alive and well, you will be very sorry.'

Denbow gave Jodie another of those disconcertingly long straight looks and did not answer. Instead he turned back to his console and operated several switches. Over his shoulder Jodie saw the needles on several gauges move in response, but she could not read the lettering on them and it meant nothing to her.

There was a metallic clanging sound from the airlock, one conveyed by steel to the air in the cabin. A moment later Jodie saw Sanderson through the side window. He waved and continued on past the vehicle toward the Probe. He was holding a portable propulsion unit in one hand, guiding himself by positioning it in relation to his body.

As she watched, he got it out of alignment with his center of gravity and went into a low spin.

Sanderson immediately cut power and straightened his body. He continued to revolve slowly as he moved through space, but he was still headed for the Probe. He hit it somewhat harder than planned and started to bounce away. Fortunately, his feet were toward the silvery skin, and he managed to swing them down and make contact. The magnetic shoes locked him in place, and he straightened up. His arms were swinging wildly in an effort to stop his involuntary body revolution; he lost the hand propulsion unit. Jodie saw it drifting away into space.

She heard a sound behind her and realized she had been watching Sanderson too long. Jodie swung both her head and body, the left hand gripping a protruding pipe for balance, the right bringing up the little pistol. Denbow was already in the air toward her, face set in a strained expression, hands reaching to knock the gun away.

Jodie had time to think that the choice was stark and simple. Shoot, and face a possible murder charge from which not even her father could save her—or let him reach her and know the struggle was over, and she had lost. There was no way she could fight this man in the environment for which only he had been trained.

Jodie pulled the trigger.

* * *

Jarl waited until he heard the astronaut actually tapping on the nose, then depressed the rod that extended the central shaft and hatch. He had struggled into his spacesuit—an awkward job without help—when the Big Bird started its final approach.

Whatever the reason for this unexpected meeting, it had better be good. When he had realized he would have to exhaust all his breathing air, he had examined his bottled supply. As best Jarl could tell, there was enough to refill the compartment one more time. It had been growing somewhat foul, and he had been thinking it was again time to dump part of it and release some more fresh oxygen. But having to pressurize from zero once more would leave him little safety margin.

It occurred to Jarl that perhaps that was the reason for this unplanned interception. Someone could have miscalculated and figured he was too short of oxygen to make it without help. If so, it seemed odd that the astronaut had not brought a bottle with him. They knew Jarl had entered with plenty of food and water. But if they were not bringing him oxygen, what in the world could have justified losing the small fortune represented by that Big Bird outside?

Although pressure in the Probe was low, it was still enough to send the air rushing out with respectable speed. Jarl stopped the hatch with it barely cracked, afraid the stream might hit the man and blow him away. And he again tried his radio, as he had several times already. Evidently his batteries were weak, though they should not have been. There was certainly no reason for the astronaut to not answer.

When the air was gone, Jarl opened the hatch the rest of the way. A moment later a helmeted head slid into view from above. Through the faceplate Jarl saw the man wore a heavy black beard—most unusual for an astronaut. The man crawled the rest of the way inside, then straightened up. He saw the shaft with the handgrips and clamped his legs around it. As Jarl watched, the astronaut zipped open a pocket on his leg—and withdrew a gun.

'Mr. Hentson, I'm very sorry, but you will have to come with me. Please don't offer any resistance. I will shoot if I must.'

For a moment Jarl thought with stunned wonder he was back in the dreamworld that had haunted him so much lately. This had to be a figment of his imagination, some childish drama that had impressed itself on the memory of his grandson. He had been aroused from lethargy and a half-dreaming condition over an hour ago when he first spotted the approaching spaceship. Somehow the adrenalin generated by excitement had revived his grip on reality, bringing back all his faculties; or so he had thought.

No, this was real. Jarl shook off the feeling of uncertainty and tongued his mike on. 'What in the world is this? Who are you, and why are you here? And why did you refuse to answer, if you could hear me calling you!'

The bearded man smiled. 'I declined to talk with you because we didn't have a good cover story prepared, Mr. Hentson. That's one of the several details we overlooked. But silence worked just as well. Now I am going to move to one side, and you are to pass me and exit out of the hatch. Don't touch any of the controls. I want those engines left off.'

'But—but *why?* What could you possibly gain? And why do you want to deprive Earth of the Probe?'

'That's a long story, Mr. Hentson. Let's just say I belong to a different school of thought. I've tried both sides and decided the one for which I was formally educated is heading in the wrong direction. But we can discuss philosophy on the way back home. Now come ahead, please. And if you want your grandson's body back on Earth safe and well, don't force me to put a bullet through it.'

'You seem to be in charge.' Jarl moved to the central shaft and started pulling himself slowly along it. The bearded man released his grip and moved a safe distance away, waiting for Jarl to pass.

At the hatch Jarl turned over and pulled himself out and up with his back to the shaft. He had seen the other man following behind him. Outside, Jarl clamped his shoes to the rounded wall and took four fast steps around the circumference of the opening. He had guessed correctly. His captor emerged from the bottom, moving quickly. He wanted to be in the open and away from Jarl before he could be reached. The gun was still held in one gloved hand.

Jarl felt his heart pounding hard. He was in complete possession of his mind, the excitement and stimulation having overcome the tendency toward troublesome intrusions from the memories of his grandson.

The second man came out with his stomach toward the shaft, expecting to find his captive in sight on the opposite side. Instead, Jarl was behind him. He chopped hard at the wrist behind the gun and connected. The weapon spun away. The man made a frantic grab for it with his other hand, missed, flailed wildly with his foot, seeking a grip—and hit the extended hatch. The impact threw him into a spin and a low drift away from the opening, his body revolving rapidly around its own center of gravity. And he was moving directly away from the two spaceships.

'Help! I can't stop! I'm—'

Jarl started to launch himself after the other man, then hesitated. Neither of these suits had a self-contained propulsive system. Unless there was an alert pilot on the Big Bird, they could both drift away and never be found.

'Listen to me! Listen!' Jarl almost yelled into his mike. 'Take off your left glove! Quickly now, take it off! Scrape the inner hand seal against your urine outlet until you have a leak! Hurry, you can do it! Stop your spin, and then you can straighten your body and use the leak like a jet to push you back here. Control the flow by pinching if off with your right hand.'

'I—I can't!' a helpless wail came back. 'I'm trying but the glove won't come off! I—how do you do this with one hand? *Help me!'*

Jarl started to rip his own glove off but stopped again. The procedure he had just given was not included in in any handbook; it had emerged strictly from rugged experience. The younger man—who was obviously an astronaut—seemed incapable of putting it into effect. But the air supply in Jarl's tanks was very low. He would be lucky to reach the slowly receding figure, much less get back.

'I can't come after you! No air! Now do as I said! Get that glove off and scrape a hole. Hurry, before you get dizzy.'

'I'm . . . already dizzy! I'm trying, but I can't—'

'Hello in the Big Bird! Can you hear me? There had not been a single response from the other vehicle, but Jarl had to try. 'A lost man is drifting out of control, almost directly away from the sun. Can you go after him? Over.'

But there was no answer. For all Jarl could tell, the bearded man might have been on board the other ship alone.

15

Tuesday, June 28, 2011

Jodie was not alone, but Denbow was unconscious. The bullet had grazed his skull, plowing a shallow furrow across the bone. She had been shooting at his head and almost missed the moving target. The lead slug had gone on past him and smashed into the pilot's console. By some unlucky freak of chance it had hit a main power supply and created a terrible short circuit. The cabinet had sputtered, several arcs had flashed—and the lights went out. When they came on again only certain widely scattered bulbs were burning, obviously from batteries.

By ripping her coverall to pieces, Jodie managed to fashion rough but serviceable bandages. She packed the bloody crease with cloth, then tied rags around his head. The material soaked through with blood, but then the flow seemed to stop. Denbow remained unconscious; his breathing was loud and ragged.

Jodie had seen wounded people before, at more than one demonstration. Denbow was suffering from shock. If he was kept warm and left alone for a few hours he would probably survive.

The air in the little compartment was foul with smoke, but the emergency fans were slowly clearing it away. When she was convinced Denbow would live, Jodie left him long enough to examine the console. You did not have to be an engineer to see the damage was extensive. If this was the only system on board capable of controlling the spaceship, it would never move under its own power again.

Jodie had tried to watch Sanderson as he went after Jarl. She had seen the brief fight outside the Probe's hatch and watched the young engineer slowly revolve away into space. Somehow she sensed when Jarl was trying to call the Big Bird on his radio, and she looked helplessly at the console. There was probably a separate emergency communications system somewhere, but she did not know how to operate it. She went to the front window and tried to signal to him, but the angle of light on the glass outside was wrong and he could not see her.

There was nothing she could do but try to keep Denbow warm and wait until God Hentson decided on his next move.

That didn't take long. She watched the spacesuited figure launch himself from the Probe's silver nose and drift directly toward her, feet first. As he came closer she saw that for some reason he had taken off his left glove. His aim was good. She watched him land on the nose just below the window. She heard his footsteps as he walked around the hull and out of sight.

It was less than five minutes later before the inner hatch opened and God Hentson floated smoothly inside.

The emergency environmental control system had almost cleared the room of smoke. The suited figure quickly closed and tightened the inner door, reached to his helmet, released the catches—and Jodie was face to face with a dead man born again, the fabulous Jarl Hentson.

She was looking at a grown but very young man, one with a fuzz of blond hair starting above his mouth, the ragged beginning of a beard. She had heard, but even in seeing she could not believe. This was Jarl Hentson resurrected, the God of technocrats and engineers come again, the father of Jesus Hentson, and perhaps the most recently famous man in the world. It was incredible that this could be him.

And then Jarl smiled, an ironic twist of young lips, and said, 'I recognize you. You were one of the leaders of that attempt to stop the launch, the girl who wore scarlet.'

And suddenly it was all believable and very real. The voice was resonant and strong, from deep in the chest, the practiced tones of an orator. The gaze was sharp and direct. Somehow he seemed to be *concentrating* on her, giving her his undivided attention, as though they were in a room full of other people whom he was presently ignoring. And she recognized this ability of intense concentration as an attribute few people had. Most of her associates could not keep their minds on one subject for two minutes straight.

There was something overpowering in this boy/man's presence, a built-in expectation of command that exceeded mere arrogance. Harold Hentson had the same quality, to a lesser extent. They were men so absolutely sure of themselves they could afford to be democratic, without pretense or condescension. It was the indefinable quality of leadership.

'Yes, I am the "scarlet woman",' Jodie said

slowly. 'My name is . . . Sarcoma.' She saw his eyebrows raise and a quick grin come and go. 'But we can get acquainted later. Right now I want to know what happened to Sanderson. I saw him drifting out of sight. Can we go after him?'

Jarl moved easily to the pilot's console and strapped himself in the seat. He examined the burned and blackened surface, then removed an access plate and peered inside. He straightened in the chair, shaking his head. 'That's a hopeless mess. And these cargo and propellant boosters are cheaply made, without an auxiliary control system. They were intended for one-time use.'

'Then can't we go after him using the Probe? I know you can guide it and stop and start the engines.'

'I'm afraid not. The Probe was designed for long-distance navigation, where every course change has to be planned days or even weeks in advance. It isn't very maneuverable.'

Jodie was silent. She remembered that only hours earlier she and Sanderson had lain cramped in the narrow cable compartment, and she had turned on her side to keep from touching him. Now she wondered why.

'I lost contact with him when I came inside,' Jarl went on. 'Let's try to reach him on the emergency comm system.'

He released himself from the chair and pushed off to a bulkhead on the left, where a square black box mingled with the rest of the equipment. When he opened the cover Jodie saw a small headset. Jarl slipped it on, flipped two switches in the bottom of the box, and spoke into the tiny mike. He tried several times, before slowly removing the headset and replacing it.

'He doesn't answer. And this system is working, so the problem is on the other end. He's probably unconscious. I'm sorry—but I don't think there's anything we can do.'

Jodie felt the taste of bile in her throat. She had seen hurt protestors, wearing their own blood like badges of honor—but this was the first time anyone had died under her leadership.

Jarl had moved to Denbow and was examining him. The wounded man's color had improved, and he was breathing easily. Jarl checked his spacesuit carefully, apparently to see if the bullet had hit it also. The suit appeared undamaged.

'Let's get his helmet on and look for another hand maneuvering unit. And I've got to transfer your gaseous oxygen tanks. With three of us in the Probe, the present supply won't last even the two days left to Earth.'

Jodie was jerked back into an awareness of the present. As was customary with Hentsons, this man was taking charge. But she hadn't come this far and risked this much to tamely accept defeat. She drew the small pistol from the jumpsuit's side pocket and said, 'But we aren't going to the Probe, Mr. President. Those engines stay off. We're going home in *this* ship!'

Jarl looked at the gun, then raised his gaze to her face. 'That's impossible. It would take a crew of techs to replace that console and recheck the power supply. We go home in the Probe or not at all.'

Jodie was holding the pistol loosely, the muzzle pointed at Jarl's feet. The boyish but muscular figure straightened, moving toward her. She lifted the gun in warning, and he stopped two meters away.

'Somehow you don't seem the type who would commit suicide,' Jarl said, looking directly into her eyes. 'You made a good try at stopping the launch, and would have succeeded if Harold hadn't scared your friends away. But out here the choice is different. Either you put down that gun and help me transfer this man and some oxygen to the Probe—or we all stay, and we all die.'

'But if I don't, the Probe will go on past Earth. And millions of hungry people will know what I did, and FOE did, and be grateful. The money that would have gone into analyzing this silver monster will be spent on food, and shelter, and medicine, the things people really need. I can't deprive them of that by letting you take it back.'

Jarl was still staring intently at her, and Jodie felt her resolution stiffen. He saw the change in her face and smiled, an expression that seemed somehow sad and aged, out of place on that young face.

'Sarcoma, as you call yourself . . . are you so convinced of your rightness that you'd die for this cause? Can't you tell yourself that once back on Earth you could still work against the Probe? That you could pressure WorldGov to hold spending on it to a minimum each year? Why do you have to adopt an either/or attitude? Life isn't that simple, and certainly human society isn't. Why sacrifice yourself when it isn't really necessary? You could achieve the same ends just as well alive.'

The proposal was alluringly attractive, logical enough to be almost believable—and ultimately, false. If this thing ahead of them got back to Earth, in twenty years Man would be sending copies of it to the stars. Jodie did not believe what she had heard about radio communications and an exchange of knowledge across the depths of space. That would put too few people to work and too little money in the pockets of space contractors and their government collaborators.

Jodie remembered a bitter lesson she had learned in college from a teacher who was a founder of FOE. It was the answer to a simple question, one he had posed to the class. 'What was the *real* purpose of the tremendous expenditures by the US government in the 1950s and '60s in the field of public housing?' The answers had ranged from the standard humanitarian considerations to an effort to defuse a budding revolution. The teacher had smilingly listened to them and then said, 'No, those were secondary reasons. The *main* drive behind public housing was the desire of a lot of contractors to make money *building* it! The actual *use* of the housing was not important, at least not to anyone with political power. And we all know the result—instant slums, to be torn down in a few years when they began crumbling around the tenants' heads. When government money is dispensed, *somebody* always makes a profit.'

And so it would be with the Probe. The aerospace industry would benefit at the expense of the rest of the world, and Jesus Hentson would grow even richer and more powerful. Perhaps he too would make President some day—or WorldGov Premier, now that the higher office existed.

'Sorry, but I don't believe you,' Jodie said, keeping the gun pointed at his broad chest. 'This game is going to be lost or won right here. And I think you've lost.'

'It isn't a game. Perhaps that's the difference between us; you think it is. But you're right that it must be settled here. Do you know what I really am? A persona imposed on the brain of a hopelessly retarded grandson?'

Jodie nodded.

'But you probably don't know that I'm already dying slowly. That's right, the grip I have on this brain is starting to fade. I give myself maybe three more days, and then I'll lose control. The body's original mind is still there, but it never reached much above the idiot level. Young Jarl's mother would miss him, and his father—but if someone has to die . . . Hal wanted to try it himself. Since he wasn't qualified he sent the two Jarls. We're highly expendable.'

'What are you getting at?' Jodie asked sharply.

'Just this. If you're going to kill us all, you may as well do it now. Shoot me, and kill the pilot there while he's still out, as an act of mercy. Then put a bullet through your own brain. Don't put the barrel to your temple, that's the amateur's way. It might not be fatal with such a small caliber. Hold the barrel in your mouth, just behind the edge of the front palate, and shoot straight up.'

Jodie shuddered. His description, and the thought, were more repulsive than the act itself would be.

'No thanks. Let's just wait until the air gives out and go quietly.'

'Sorry, I won't allow you that. You are either going to have to shoot, or give me the gun. Now I am going to pull myself to you along this wall. If I reach you, I am going to take the pistol. Then I'll try to save us all. It won't be easy because we're running out of time, and I think we'll be short one spacesuit.'

Jarl reached for the wall, caught a projection, and began slowly and calmly pulling himself toward Jodie. She raised the pistol to eye-level, took careful aim at his head—and froze, suspended in time, the confined world of the pilot's compartment sharp and bright and clear around her. There was no hurry. She had subjective hours in which to squeeze the trigger.

And to make up her mind.

God Hentson had gotten to her, after all. She did not want to die. She had managed to shoot the pilot when he jumped her, knowing it might mean prison later—but her own life was not immediately at stake. Now it was. And the hard and pressing question was: did she believe in her cause strongly enough to die for it?

There was a chance Jarl Hentson would turn back. He was coming toward her with the relentless calmness and certainty of one of the giant machines he represented. This was not a contest of wills between them—his was implacable. It was a test of hers alone. If she believed, she must pull that trigger.

Jodie concentrated on the tension against her finger, the fragile resistance of oiled steel, the tiny bit of added pressure needed—and Jarl slowly and carefully reached for the pistol and pulled it from her hand.

Jodie let it go and turned and faced the wall. For the first time since she was twelve years old, she felt like crying . . . but she didn't.

* * *

Jarl returned to the Probe by the same method he had left it—carefully pointing his body in the right direction and pushing off with his arms. He still had his left glove off just in case but did not have to create the emergency maneuvering system he had outlined to Sanderson. His aim was again good, and he landed near the hatch.

Jarl untied the end of the electrical wire around

his waist, pulled it taut, and secured it to the door shaft. The wire was the heaviest gauge he had been able to rip free. Then he crossed back by it and entered the crippled Big Bird's airlock. Operating the closing mechanism by hand was a nuisance, but he endured it.

Inside, he saw with approval that Jodie—he had refused to continue calling her Sarcoma—had Denbow ready to go. He checked the unconscious man's air supply himself and then told her to start getting into one of the four spacesuits they had found listed in the cargo manifest. That, at least, had been a bit of good luck. The fact he had thought to check indicated his brain was still in good working order.

The airlock was only intended for one person at the time, but Jarl managed to squeeze in with Denbow. Pulling the limp body of the pilot along the wire was tricky, but the trip was short. When Denbow was safely inside, Jarl hurried back. He was in time to help Jodie on with her helmet and to verify that the attached back-pack had plenty of oxygen.

So did the other three tanks, which Jarl had separated from the packs. Why they had been shipped pressurized, when they could as well have been sent empty and filled from the space station's liquid oxygen conversion unit, was a question to take up later with the RI Safety Office. For now, they were the only supply of easily transportable oxygen on board the Big Bird. Jarl did not have the equipment needed to remove liquid oxygen from the propellant tank, nor to free and transfer the large bottles supplying the pilot's compartment.

'How long do we have before you need to start decelerating the Probe again?' Jodie asked over the radio as she followed him outside. Now that she was committed to living, Jodie seemed as anxious about her prospects as anyone else.

'I don't know exactly. This is seat-of-the-pants navigation. I'd have tried to get some updates from Earth if you hadn't ruined the radio. The emergency comm system won't reach that far. Now when you grasp the wire, pull very gently, and remember you'll keep moving once you've started. Don't build up much speed.'

Jodie did as she was told and reached the Probe safely. She hesitated before crawling into the narrow opening behind the round door but made it inside.

Jarl waited at the airlock until Jodie vanished, and then started across. He had the three tanks clasped under one arm, a bulky but not difficult load. But he miscalculated his momentum because of the extra mass, and his feet slammed against the round hatch harder than he had intended. The jar was not enough to cost him his grip on the precious oxygen.

With his cargo safely inside, Jarl untied the heavy wire. He was outside the Probe, with his bent knees locked over the door's edge. He formed a loop in the heavy line as far out as he could reach, gripped it in both hands, and pulled with all his might. Nothing happened. He kept up the pressure for two minutes, every muscle in his strong young body trembling with effort—and very slowly and gradually the pressure eased as the line moved, slipping almost imperceptibly toward him.

Jarl cast the line away, toward the Big Bird, and hurried inside and down the shaft. At the peculiar control station he activated the mechanism that pulled the hatch closed, watching the other spaceship through his right outside camera. It was moving toward them with slow but massive inevitability. They were going to bump.

Jarl glanced at Jodie and Denbow. She was crouched over the still unconscious man, watching his face. Earlier she had tried to kill him. Now that he was alive, she was intensely concerned over his health.

And somehow Jarl could not think it was simply because of the difference between a murder charge and one of attempted murder and armed robbery. She was honestly worried about the man she had shot.

'Move back to the rear wall and lay Denbow flat against it,' Jarl said over his radio. 'This bird doesn't accelerate very fast, but he should be spared all the strain we can save him.'

Jodie nodded, and pulled her patient along like a balloon behind her. At the rear she found a clear flat space—the back wall was not as cluttered with equipment and instruments as the others—and grasped a projection to steady herself while she held Denbow in place with her legs.

Jarl looked back at the screen. The nose of the Big Bird has almost reached them, looming enormous only a few meters ahead of the camera eye. And a minute later there was a solid but subdued bump, and the Probe's front started slowly rising. The more pointed nose of the Earth cargo carrier had hit them just below the hatch, as Jarl had calculated. It was angling beneath the round silver belly and would eventually pass beneath.

But Jarl did not wait. The Probe's rockets could conceivably be hit and damaged. When the tilt reached the point where the other ship became lost to the camera, he depressed the engine-start rod.

The Probe's engines came alive with blue fury, and there was almost instant gravity inside. The ship sliding beneath them was hit by the exhaust and started a slow spin—Jarl saw it by slanting the rear camera downward to its limit—but it no longer mattered. The Probe was gone long before the other ship's tail passed through the space where it had been.

If the Probe had small attitude engines like those on the Big Bird, this maneuver would not have been necessary. But as he had told Jodie, the gnomes had designed it for one purpose only, and maneuverability was not needed. In fact he had yet to learn any means of operating the engines other than at full power. But the nozzles could be tilted slightly, which was how the Probe guided itself.

Jarl turned off the engines after a few minutes and hunted with the rear camera until he found Earth. It took him two more sightings to regain his former attitude and make a slight change in angle of approach. He had to work in three hours of deceleration they had lost here, performing all calculations in his head. But when the sun was finally directly ahead and the Earth behind and well to the left of center, he felt satisfied again. This was crude navigation, but he had plenty of time over the next forty-eight hours in which to crank in corrections.

And then he set about opening the values on the last of his original supply of oxygen, wondering how long it was going to sustain three people, and if it would even reach the minimum pressure needed to assure good breathing.

After an hour passed he knew the oxygen pressure was satisfactory and felt certain the amount in the back-pack tanks could freshen it enough to keep them alive.

Unless they were going to miss the Earth entirely, a possibility Jarl could not ignore. He refused to let the thought worry him.

16

Thursday, June 30, 2011

Harold turned away from his desk screen and let it sink out of sight. Along with a large portion of the rest of the world, he had just watched a Space Shuttle intercept the Probe at perigee on its second Earth orbit. WWN had carried the event live.

A highly experienced SB pilot was now in the Probe, and he had been supplied not only with oxygen and food but a hastily installed radio. The orbit would be circularized and lowered, prepatory to bringing the Probe alongside the Space Station. After that it would be turned over to the world's scientists and engineers for study.

Harold glanced at the court order still lying on his desk, the only piece of paper there. He specifically, and RI as a corporation, was ordered to hand over custody of the Probe to authorized representatives of the Space Benefits Agency. And this time there was no way to fight the government. Not that he wanted to. The three days he had spent in jail had taught Harold what to fear and dread—confinement and helplessness. Not willingly would he go behind bars again.

And of course he had expected all along that WorldGov would take the Probe away once it reached Earth. It would have been uncharacteristic of government in general to have behaved otherwise. RI's countersuit was already in court, and the eventual terms of settlement would assure them a continued role of leadership in the aerospace industry.

Harold was more worried over Jarl. He had seen him give a casual wave to the TV camera, but his son/father had refused to speak to newsmen on the Shuttle. And he had made a strange request of the doctor on board—that he be put to sleep and not be awakened until he was safely back at the RI laboratory where he had been 'treated'.

According to Pepi's best estimates, it was now time for the persona of Jarl senior to be fading away. The only answer that made sense was that this was happening and that the old man did not want to betray his mental confusion.

Harold had a sudden thought and reached to punch his visicom button. 'Pat, have someone get over to my place and bring Lily here. Tell her we're going to meet Jarl when he arrives.'

SB had swiftly agreed to RI's request for custody of Jarl. They did not want to be responsible for him. He was to be under Pepi's care during his recovery from the imprinting.

The landing of the Shuttle and the removal of the three special passengers were not televised. But it was less than two hours from the time Harold had turned off his screen before he left his office to meet the ambulance aircar on the roof. Lily was already up there patiently waiting.

To Harold's surprise, he saw Jodie Carson get off the aircar with the stretcher holding the sleeping Jarl. The third passenger, Denbow, had been taken to the Space Center medical facility to have his head wound properly treated.

Lily rushed forward to stand with hands clasped over the unconscious body of her son. She was trying hard to hold back the tears. As the two medical attendants rolled their patient toward the elevator, Jodie following, Harold fell into step beside her. A man he did not know walked a few paces behind them.

'I'm under arrest,' Jodie said by way of greeting, pointing to the man following her. 'But I convinced the top WorldGov guard-dog at the landing strip I had some medical info on Jarl, so they let me come along.'

'Do you?' Harold asked.

'Oh, definitely. For one thing, the persona fades almost completely now when Jarl is sleepy or inactive. Even when he's wide awake, the mind is very shaky unless the body is active or excited. While he was placing us in orbit I had to keep yelling at him —insults or obscenities and such—to make him angry.'

In the lab, Pepi and the company doctor carefully examined Jarl. After talking with Jodie, they decided to awaken him but without using a stimulant. After a gentle shaking, Jarl sat up in the stretcher and smiled at them. He yawned, hands high over his head, and sighed. He looked at Lily and, in a voice filled with love, said, 'Hello, Mommy.'

Harold could hardly believe his ears. This was certainly not his father speaking—but neither was it his idiot son!

Lily gasped; the shock was almost too much for her. The tears that had been leaking from her eyes swelled to a flood, and she ran to clasp Jarl in her arms before the medics could stop her. Pepi motioned for them to leave her alone, and Lily buried her face on her son's broad chest.

'As I was saying earlier,' Jodie said to Pepi, 'Jarl—the imprint, that is—told me he felt the subordinate mind coming back into control, taking over more and more of the body's functions. But he also said the other mind seemed to be stronger now, as though perhaps new neural pathways had been opened. He was having complete, coherent thoughts that were not really his own and felt they had to be from young Jarl. It was his opinion he would fade away completely after a time, but the mind wouldn't revert back to its original state. Oh, before I forget, he also said he had noticed all along he was receiving his grandson's *emotions,* that any time he thought about Harold, or the boy's mother, he would get strong upwellings of feeling that he knew weren't really his. It was the persona Jarl's hope that the problem with young Jarl's mind, whatever it was, had been cured and that he could lead a normal life now. He said you were to run some basic intelligence tests as soon as the imprint was completely gone and see if young Jarl's mind didn't seem capable of learning. He felt certain it would be.'

'I'm beginning to think so myself!' Pepi said, his voice growing excited. 'I wonder—could this imprint technique be modified to cure other cases of retardation, where there's no organic damage? This could open up a whole new field of medicine!'

Harold had to repress the inclination to chuckle aloud. That was a good RI scientist talking. But it wasn't really their line of business, and Pepi's work would have to be turned over to some organization better capable of developing this fresh start. He wondered if he would lose Pepi when it happened.

'Can I have just a moment alone with this criminal?' Harold asked the quiet security man following Jodie.

The officer shrugged. 'Mr. Hentson, I expect you could have just about anything in the world you wanted right now. Just bring her back to me, please.'

Looking surprised, Jodie followed Harold into Pepi's office. When they were alone he placed both hands on her shoulders, staring into the dark eyes that met his in wide curiosity. 'I was wondering—' Harold hesitated, searching for the words. 'What I want to know is, has this adventure changed your feelings toward the space program? Do you still think we're a useless luxury now that you've seen what space science and technology can do? Is it possible for us to be . . . friends?'

Jodie pulled back from him, smiling in wry amusement. 'You don't want to be friends, Hal. You want a mistress—and it's a tempting thought, but it wouldn't work. The only place two strong wills like ours could agree would be in bed—and that isn't enough. Of course I'm going to keep fighting the space program. It's no more useful today than it was last year. Maybe less, because now some of the dreamers will start bigger and more wasteful projects to explore the whole galaxy. You and your father have opened up a big new playground for them.'

Harold did not try to hide his disappointment. 'I should have realized you'd still feel that way. Sorry I asked.'

Jodie's expression softened. 'Listen, Hal. We

had one good night, and that's more than most people get in their lifetimes. Settle for it. Now I have to call my lawyer and try to arrange bail. I've seen the inside of too many jails already. No, don't kiss me. Let's end it clean. The next time you see me it will be across a picket line.'

Jodie walked to the door and out.

POSTSCRIPT

'I think the space programme has been largely responsible for this surge of interest in ecology—those wonderful photographs of the planet Earth had a tremendous psychological impact. It's no coincidence that we became aware of the ecological crisis at the precise moment when we saw our beautiful green planet hanging over the lifeless moon. What we need now is not less science nor less technology, but *more* of both—but they must be carefully planned.'

Arthur C. Clarke
(From remarks made at the Trieste
Science-Fiction Film Festival,
Trieste, Italy, in July 1971; reported in
Speculation No. 29,
October 1971)